JUST ONE MORE

by Jeanne B. Hardendorff

Published by J. B. Lippincott Company

The reviewers say:

"A welcome collection of short, quick-to-tell stories
selected and retold by an experienced storyteller to
help other storytellers respond to the plea for just
one more story. . .Handy for storytelling and for
reading aloud and agreeable fare for the individual
reader. . ." Suggested for the Small Library.

---A.L.A. Booklist

". . .This collection has variety and most of the
stories will be new to the listeners. . .a boon to
have this book on the shelf. It can. . .be read
happily by children and is attractive in appearance..."

---Young Readers' Review

"For those children who always want to hear one more
story, this book is the answer. These 40 stories are
very brief and always to the point--no elaborate use
of words to fill up pages; just entertaining reading
about the follies of man and beast."

---Publishers' Weekly

JUST ONE MORE

JUST
ONE MORE

Selected and retold by
Jeanne B. Hardendorff

Illustrated by Don Bolognese

J. B. Lippincott Company

PHILADELPHIA   NEW YORK

ACKNOWLEDGMENTS

How the Chipmunk came, How the Coyote Stole Fire for the Klamaths, and *How Yehl Outwitted Kanukh and Gave Fresh Water to the Thlinkits* originally published in A BOOK OF INDIAN TALES, retold by Charles Erskine Scott Wood, copyright 1929 by The Vanguard Press.

The Bee originally published in AND IT CAME TO PASS told by Kayyim Nahman Bialik; tr. by Herbert Danby, copyright 1938 by Hebrew Publishing Co.

The Cat and the Sparrows, The Frog and the Snake, The Parrot and the Parson, The Wily Tortoise, and *The Wise Old Shepherd* were originally published in THE TALKING THRUSH by W. H. D. Rouse, copyright 1899 by J. M. Dent Co. and E. P. Dutton.

How the Fog Came and *Imarasugssuaq, Who Ate His Wives* originally published in ESKIMO FOLK TALES by Knud Rasmussen, copyright 1929 by Gyldendal.

Foolish Mother Goat, The Monkey and the Heron, The Story of Yukpachen, and *The Tiger and the Frog* originally published in THE MAGIC BIRD OF CHOMO-LUNG-MA by Sybille Noel, copyright 1931 by Doubleday, Doran and Company.

Riddles originally published in RUSSIAN FAIRY TALES edited by Norbert Guterman. Published by Pantheon, copyright 1945.

To MY SISTERS
Ca and Rene
for the days when we answered to the call,
"Jeanne-Rene-and-Catharine."

Foreword

Children ask for "just one more" story. Every storyteller needs stories which can be told quickly to satisfy the plea for more. As a storyteller I have always looked for the ones which would only take a minute or two or three so that I could tell that one additional story for the children. Sometimes I have needed a quick-to-tell story to add to a talk about books, or when I was talking to groups of children about coming to the regular library story hour— it was only fair to give a sample of what they would hear. I had to use many collections of folktales to keep a supply of the short, quick-to-tell stories fresh for telling. There was no one book I could use.

So this book of short, quick-to-tell stories is for the storytellers who need just one more. It is for the parents whose children like them to read as well as to tell them stories. And it is for the children of all the story hours because they asked for "just one more." And it is for the children who have enjoyed hearing stories and would like to read or tell stories on their own. I was such a child and well remember my early attempts at story-telling.

In the *Notes* at the end, I have given the approximate time it takes to tell each story. Out of the forty stories

in this book, only eight take more than five minutes to
tell. Twenty-three of the stories take three minutes or
less and there are four which take less than a minute.

Children ask for different kinds of stories, too. They
may want "just one more" ghost story. So there are two
ghost stories in this collection. *The Ghost Who Was
Afraid of Being Bagged* is a funny story while *Heavy
Collar and the Ghost Woman* is a powerful, eerie tale
told by the Blackfoot Indians.

If the children ask for a story that is funny, they will
find the snake wife's demands in *The Wise Old Shepherd* to their liking. The trick played on the wolf in *The
Wolf and the Blacksmith* is sure to make them laugh.

They like a story that is a struggle of wit against wit
with a bit of magic thrown in such as in *Yehl Outwits
Kanukh*, or a success story where quick thinking lets the
smaller animal get the better of the bigger more fierce
animal as in *The Tiger and the Frog*.

Then there are times when the children want to have
a part in the telling as they can in *Origin of Day and
Night*. They always like the story which ends so quickly
they are surprised and it turns out to be a joke on the
listener as in *The Tail*.

Each story has been chosen for this collection with a
particular "just one more" plea in mind for at some time
I have been asked for one like it.

Contents

❦❦❦

JUST ONE MORE

The Magpie
and Her Children

❦❦❦

THERE WAS ONCE a Magpie who said to her children:

"It's high time you learned to look for your own food; it is indeed!"

And with that she turned the whole lot of them out of their nest and took them into the fields.

But the Magpie's children didn't care about that.

"We'd rather go back to our nest!" they cried. "It's so comfortable to have you bringing our food to us in your beak!"

"I daresay!" said their mother. "But you're big enough to feed yourselves. *I* was turned out of the nest when I was much younger, I can tell you that!"

"But people will kill us with their bows and arrows," said the young magpies.

"No fear of that!" replied their mother. "People can't shoot without taking aim, and that takes time. When you see them raising the bows to their faces, ready to draw, you must just fly away."

"We might do that," said the children, "but if someone were to throw a stone at us, he wouldn't have to take aim."

"Well, you'll see him stooping down to pick up the stone," said the old Magpie.

"But supposing he carried a stone in his hand, ready?"

"Why, if you're sharp enough to think of that," said their mother, "you're sharp enough to take care of yourselves!"

And with that she flew away and left them.

The Frog and the Snake

A FROG and a Snake had a quarrel as to which could give the more deadly bite. They agreed to try it on the next opportunity.

A Man came to bathe in the pond where these two creatures lived. The Snake bit him under the water, while the Frog floated on the top.

"Something has bitten me!" the Man called out to his friends.

"What is it?" they asked.

Then he saw the Frog swimming on the top of the water.

"Oh, it's only a Frog," said he. Then he went away, and no harm came of it.

The next time that Man came to bathe in the pond, the Frog bit him under the water, while the Snake swam on the top.

"Oh, dear," said the Man, "a Snake has bitten me!" The Man died.

"Now," said the Frog, "you will admit that my bite is more poisonous than yours."

"I deny it altogether," said the Snake.

So they agreed to refer their dispute to the King of the Snakes. The Snake King listened to their arguments, and said the Man had died of fright.

"Of course," grumbled the Frog, "the Snake King sides with the Snake."

So both of them bit the Frog, and he died, and that was the end of him.

Thirty-two Teeth

❦❦❦

AN IRISHMAN was arguing with a Welshman, when the Welshman, who was quick to anger, became angry, and said:

"I have half a mind to knock out every one of your thirty-two teeth!"

The astonished Irishman left the Welshman standing there and hurried home to consult his wife.

"In heaven's name, good Wife," he said, "come here and count my teeth, for I am very anxious to know how many I have."

The Irishman's wife counted his teeth, and then said, "Indeed, Husband, I find that you have thirty-two teeth, neither more nor less."

The Irishman thought a long time about what his wife had said and then muttered to himself, "How did my friend the Welshman know I had thirty-two teeth?"

The Fox and the Icicle

❧❧❧

A HUNGRY FOX, searching for food one winter day, came across a long, fine icicle, shaped very much like a bone, and fell to gnawing it eagerly.

"A plague upon it!" said he. "There is the sound of a bone in my ears, and the feel of a bone between my teeth, but never a scrap of it goes down into my stomach!"

A Witty Answer

A CERTAIN KING was angry with one of his Lords, and put him in prison. Wishing to keep him there, he said he would only set him free if he could bring to the court a horse which was neither gray, nor black, brown nor bay, white nor roan, dun, chestnut, nor piebald—and, in short, the King enumerated every possible color that a horse could be.

The imprisoned Lord promised to get such a horse if the King would set him free at once. As soon as he was at liberty, the Lord asked the King to send a groom for the horse, but begged that the groom might come neither on Monday nor Tuesday, Wednesday nor Thursday, Friday, Saturday nor Sunday, but on any other day of the week that suited His Majesty.

Origin of Day
and Night

❦❦❦

ONE DAY as Wabus, the Rabbit, traveled through a forest, he came to a clearing on the bank of the river. There sat Totoba, the Saw-whet Owl. The light was dim and Rabbit could not see well. He said to Saw-whet, "Why do you want it so dark? I do not like it. I will cause it to be light."

Saw-whet said, "Do so, if you are strong enough. Let us try our powers."

So Rabbit and Owl called a great council of the birds and animals. Some of the birds and animals wanted Rabbit to succeed so that it would be light. Others wanted it to remain dark.

Rabbit and Owl began to try their powers. Rabbit began to repeat rapidly, "*Wabon. Wabon. Wabon.* (Light. Light. Light.) while Owl kept saying as rapidly as he could, "*Uni tipa qkot. Uni tipa qkot. Uni tipa qkot.* (Night. Night. Night.)

It had been decided that if one of them should speak the word of the other, he would lose. So Rabbit kept repeating more and more rapidly, "*Wabon. Wabon. Wabon*," while Owl said as rapidly as he could, "*Uni tipa qkot. Uni tipa qkot. Uni tipa qkot.*" At last Owl said the Rabbit's word, "*Wabon*," so he lost.

Therefore Rabbit decided there should be light. But because some of the animals and birds could hunt only in the dark, he said it should be night part of the time. But all the rest of the time it would be day.

Manabush
and the Moose

❦❦❦

MANABUSH, THE INDIAN, killed a moose. He was very hungry, but he was greatly troubled as to how he should eat it.

He looked at the moose and he began to talk to himself:

"If I begin at the head," he said, "they will say I ate him headfirst."

Then he walked around the moose until he stood opposite its side. "But if I begin at the side," he said, "they will say I ate him sideways."

The Manabush walked around the moose until he stood opposite its tail. "And if I begin at the tail," he said to himself, "they will say I ate him tail first."

He was greatly troubled. And while he considered his problem, the wind blew two tree branches together. It made a harsh, creaking sound.

"I cannot eat in this noise," said Manabush, and he climbed the tree. Immediately the branches caught him by the arm and held him. Then a pack of wolves came and ate up the moose.

The Box with Something Pretty in It

ONCE UPON A TIME there was a little Boy who was out walking on the road, and when he had walked a bit he found a box.

"I am sure there must be something pretty in this box," he said to himself; but however much he turned it, and however much he twisted it, he was not able to get it open.

But when he had walked a bit farther, he found a little tiny key. Then he grew tired and sat down, and all at once he thought what fun it would be if the key fitted the box, for it had a little keyhole in it. So he took the little key out of his pocket, and then he blew first into the pipe of the key, and afterward into the keyhole, and then he put the key into the keyhole and turned it. "Snap!" it went within the lock; and when he tried the hasp, the box was open.

But can you guess what there was in the box?
Why, a cow's tail; and if the cow's tail had been
longer, this story would have been longer, too.

The Arab
and His Camel

THERE WAS ONCE an Arab who, when he had finished loading his camel, turned to him and asked,

"My friend Camel, do you prefer to go uphill or downhill?"

"Pray, Master," said the Camel dryly, "Is the *straight* way across the plain closed to travelers?"

The Tail

🌷🌷🌷

THERE WAS A Shepherd once who went out to the hill to look after his sheep. It was misty and cold, and he had much trouble to find them. At last he had them all but one; and after much searching he found that one, too, in a peat bog, half drowned; so he took off his plaid, and bent down and took hold of the sheep's tail and he pulled.

The sheep was heavy with water, and he could not lift her, so he took off his coat and he *pulled!!*

But it was too much for him, so he spit on his hands, and took a good hold of the tail and he PULLED!—and the tail broke!

And if it had not been for that this tale would have been a great deal longer.

Foolish Mother Goat

OLD MOTHER GOAT had for a long time been envious of the sheep who had nice soft curly coats, and whose lambs skipped about in all weathers with nice fluffy coats, too. Her coat was coarse, and as for her kid, his coat was coarse also, and in rainy weather they both looked positive frights with their hair all wet and straight and draggled.

One fine day a little lamb strayed from his mother, and being afraid, he made for Mother Goat and snuggled up to her. She gave the lamb a warm drink, and he slept at her side all the morning with her own kid. Mother Goat dozed herself, and when she woke up her kid and the lamb were frisking together.

Mother Goat had a poor memory so far as her children were concerned. She had brought up a numerous family. She watched the two young things frisking and playing their games and noticed that one had a fleecy woolly coat. She blinked and then swelled up with pride.

"At last," said Mother Goat, "I have a child with a soft curly coat," and she shouted for Old Father Goat, who was busy munching, to come at once.

"Look there," said Old Mother Goat, "now, you see, we have a child with fluffy, curly hair. I always knew that my great-grandmother was a sheep."

Father Goat was a bit surprised.

"Without doubt," said Mother Goat, ready to burst with pride, "I am a quarter sheep."

"You don't look it," said Father Goat, "you look a thorough goat."

"What are you saying?" said Mother Goat

crossly. "If my great-grandmother was a sheep, I must be a quarter sheep."

"I don't believe your great-grandmother was a sheep," said Father Goat.

"Well," said Mother Goat, "perhaps you will tell me how it has come about that I have a child that looks like a lamb."

Father Goat racked his brains, but he could not think for the life of him. "If your great-grandmother was a sheep," said Father Goat, "and you are a quarter sheep—that would make the lamb less than a quarter sheep."

"But you can see," said Mother Goat, "that it is a pure lamb. How can you answer that?"

This was altogether too much for Father Goat. He couldn't answer.

"I thought as much," said Mother Goat. "You can't answer." Thereupon Father Goat lost his temper, made Mother Goat lose hers, and they raised their voices to such a pitch that the Kid and the Lamb frisked up to see what all the bother was about.

"How is it," said Father Goat, "that one of you has straight hair and the other curly hair?"

"Why haven't I got curly hair?" said the Kid to the Lamb.

"Because I'm different," said the Lamb.

"Keep quiet," said Mother Goat. "You have

curly hair because you are a lamb, and because your great-great-grandmother was a sheep."

Just then the Old Sheep came over the slope of the hill. "That's my mother," said the Lamb, and he ran to her, and the two disappeared over the side of the hill.

"Where's my son?" screamed Mother Goat.

"Here he is," said Father Goat, butting the kid.

"I mean the other one," said Mother Goat. "The one with curly hair."

"His mother," said Father Goat, "is a sheep."

"Ah!" said Mother Goat. "So now you will admit I was more than right. Tell me, if my great-grandmother was a sheep, and my one son is a lamb, would that make me a pure sheep?"

But Father Goat was too exhausted to answer. He lay with his tongue hanging dry and his eyes nearly popping out of their sockets, while Mother Goat said over and over again, "I always knew I was a sheep."

The Most Frugal
of Men

❦❦❦

A Man who was considered the most frugal of all the dwellers in a certain kingdom heard of another Man who was the most frugal in the whole world.

He said to his son: "We, indeed, live upon little, but if we were more frugal still, we might live upon nothing at all. It might be well worthwhile for us to get instruction in thrift from the Most Frugal of Men."

The Son agreed, and the two decided that the Son should go and inquire whether the Most Frugal of Men would take pupils.

It was the custom in that kingdom to exchange presents before any business was to be transacted. So the Father told the Son to take the smallest of coins, one penny, and to buy a sheet of paper of the cheapest sort.

The Son, by bargaining, got two sheets of paper for the penny. The Father put away one sheet, cut the other sheet in halves, and on one half drew a small picture of a pig's head. This he put into a large covered basket, as if it were a real pig's head —the usual gift sent in token of great respect. The Son took the basket, and after a long journey reached the house of the Most Frugal Man in the World.

The Man himself was absent, but his Son received the traveler, learned his errand, and accepted the offering. Having taken from the basket the picture of the pig's head, he said courteously to his visitor: "I am sorry that we have nothing in the house that is worthy to take the place of the pig's head in your basket. I will, however, show our friendly reception of it by putting in four oranges for you to take home with you."

Thereupon the young Man, without having any oranges at hand, made the motions necessary for putting the fruit into the basket. The Son of the most frugal man in the kingdom then took the basket and went to his father to tell of thrift surpassing his own.

When the Most Frugal Man in the World returned home, his Son told him that a visitor had been there, having come from a great distance to take lessons in economy. The Father inquired what offering he brought as an introduction, and the Son showed the small outline of the pig's head on thin brown paper.

The Father looked at it and then asked his son what he had sent as a return present. The Son told him he had merely made the motions necessary for transferring four oranges, and showed how he had clasped the imaginary fruit and deposited it in the visitor's basket.

The Father immediately flew into a terrible rage and boxed the boy's ears, exclaiming: "You extravagant wretch! With your fingers thus far apart you appeared to give him large oranges. Why didn't you measure out small ones?"

The Crow
and the Peacock

🌷🌷🌷

ONE DAY the Peacock said to the Crow:

"This is Lord Tiger's wedding day. How shall we adorn ourselves for the wedding?"

At that time the Crow was white and the Peacock yellow like a hen.

"I have an idea!" the Crow replied. "The King of Annam is having a house built. It is a wonderful house! The walls are being decorated with all the colors of the rainbow. There are dragons that are green and red, yellow and blue. The workmen have gone to eat their luncheon. We will run and get their pots of paint."

The Crow immediately put his idea into execution.

The Peacock insisted upon being painted first.

The Crow, wishing to show his ability, painted upon the Peacock's feathers moons of yellow and green, arabesques of blue and black.

The Peacock was magnificent. He went to look at himself in the water of the river, spreading out his tail to dry his feathers. But when he saw that he was so handsome he continued to spread his tail, even after his feathers were dry.

"Kwong-toh! Kwong-toh! How beautiful I am! How beautiful I am!"

Just then the Crow called to him: "Friend, it is your turn to show your cleverness!"

But the Peacock was proud and jealous. He had no intention of decorating the Crow for Lord Tiger's wedding. So he said:

"Didn't you hear the cry of that eagle? We must fly! We must hide ourselves!"

And, pretending a great haste, he ran against

the pots of paint and knocked them into the river.

"I did not hear an eagle cry," said the Crow.

"Then, I must have been mistaken. Come, I will paint you."

"The paint is at the bottom of the river," the Crow said.

"But here is one pot," said the Peacock.

"Then hurry!" replied the Crow.

"There! You look lovely!" exclaimed the Peacock.

The Crow went to look at himself in the water of the river—and found that he had been cruelly deceived. He wished to complain; but his voice choked in his throat, and he could only scream harshly: "Caw! Caw!"

Ever since then Crows have been black and have had a harsh voice; while Peacocks are made gorgeous with a thousand colors.

But their voice is no better for all that!

The Shepherd Boy Who Was Wiser Than the King

❧❧❧

ONCE UPON A TIME there was a Shepherd Boy who was famed far and wide for the wise answers which he gave to all questions. Now the King of the country heard of this boy, but he would not believe what was said about him, so the Shepherd Boy was ordered to come to court.

When he arrived the King said to him: "If you can give me answers to each of the three questions which I will now put to you, I will bring you up as my own child, and you shall live here with me in my palace."

"What are these three questions?" asked the Boy.

"The first is: How many drops of water are there in the sea?"

"My lord King," replied the Shepherd Boy, "let all the waters be stopped up on the earth, so that not one drop shall run into the sea before I count it, and then I will tell you how many drops there are in the sea!"

"The second question," said the King, "is: How many stars are there in the sky?"

"Give me a large sheet of paper," said the Boy. And then he made so many minute holes in the paper with a pin that they were far too numerous to see or to count, and dazzled the eyes of whomever looked at them. When he had finished, he said: "There are as many stars in the sky as there are holes in this paper; now count them." But nobody was able.

Thereupon the King said: "The third question is: How many seconds are there in eternity?"

"In Lower Pomerania is located the Adamantine mountain, one mile in height, one mile in breath, and one mile deep; and to this mountain comes a bird once in every thousand years which rubs its beak against one certain hill, and, when the whole mountain shall be rubbed away, then will the first second of eternity be gone by."

"You have answered the three questions like a sage," said the King, "and from henceforward you shall live with me in my palace, and I will treat you as my own child."

How the Chipmunk Came to Be

A LONG TIME AGO there lived among these islands an old Demon Hag. She had terrible teeth like a dog's and terrible claws like a cougar's. She lived on the children of the people. She would wait for them in the dark paths of the woods or on the edge of the village at nightfall, and would pounce upon them and tear them and eat them. All the people were afraid and the land was filled with crying mothers and frightened children.

There was one Mother that had a little Boy; very fat, very bright eyes, and laughing all the time. She loved her son very much and prayed the Great Spirit to save him from the old Demon Hag.

One day they had been out fishing together; and as they were hurrying home, the little Boy walking in front of his mother, there came a horrible sound, and the great skinny Devil Woman swooped down on the child as a hawk does on a field mouse. Then the Mother's heart became sick, but she put her hands and face up to the Great Spirit and prayed him to save her boy.

The Great Spirit heard her cry and changed the little boy into a chipmunk, but the old witch's claws had already streaked his side.—The marks are there to this day.

Then the Mother fixed up a dog to look like a child and put it one evening on the edge of the path; and she went into the bushes a step and cried like a child. The Old Hag came flying through the air and seized the dog, tearing and eating it before she knew; but dog meat is bad medicine for a witch, so she fell on the ground, groaning. Then the Mother built a fire around her and burnt her up.

The chipmunk became very small and went with his mother everywhere, talking to her; but now they have forgotten how to talk.

This is the way the chipmunk came to be.

The Best of
the Bargain

THERE ONCE LIVED in the city of Bagdad, during the reign of the Caliph Haroun Er Raschid, a famous barber whose name was Ali Sakal. He was so expert in his manner of shaving that all the great men of Bagdad employed him. This made him so vain and insolent that at length he would scarcely shave anyone who was not rich and noble.

It happened one day that a poor Woodcutter, who did not know what kind of man Ali Sakal was, went to his shop, and offered a load of wood for sale. Ali Sakal, who needed wood, immediately promised him a price *for all the wood that was on his donkey.*

The Woodcutter agreed to this bargain, unloaded his beast, and asked for the money.

"You have not given me all the wood yet," said the Barber. "I must have the packsaddle (which was made mostly of wood) into the bargain; that was our agreement."

"Now," said the other in great amazement, "whoever heard of such a bargain? It is impossible!" But in spite of all the poor man's remonstrances the overbearing barber seized packsaddle, wood, and all, and sent away the peasant in great distress.

The poor man ran immediately to the Cadi, and stated his griefs, but the Cadi was a friend of the barber, and refused to hear the case. The Woodcutter applied to a higher Judge, and he, too, was a friend of the barber, and made light of the matter. He then appealed to the Mufti himself, with the like result.

The poor man, however, was not discouraged, but sent a petition to the Caliph Haroun Er Raschid, who promptly summoned the Woodcutter before him.

The Woodcutter hastened to present himself, and kissed the ground before the throne, and then awaited the Caliph's decision.

"My friend," said the Caliph, "the Barber has words upon his side,—you have equity on yours. The law must be defined by words, and agreements must be made by words. Agreements *must* be kept, or there would be no faith between man and man. Therefore, the Barber must keep all the wood; but—" then calling the Woodcutter close to him, the Caliph whispered something in his ear, which none but he could hear and the poor man went away satisfied.

A few days after this the Woodcutter went to the Barber, and, as if nothing had happened, asked him to shave his head, and also his companion who waited without. The Barber, pleased to think that he had go off so easily in the affair of the wood, agreed to shave them both.

The Woodcutter immediately went out and returned leading his donkey behind him by the halter. "This is my companion," said he, "and you must shave him."

"Shave him!" exclaimed the Barber. "Is it not enough that I have demeaned myself by promising to touch you; that now you insult me by asking me to shave your donkey! Away with you!" and he drove them both out of his shop.

The Woodcutter ran straightway to the Caliph, was admitted to his presence, and stated his case.

"It is well!" said the Commander of the Faithful. "Bring Ali Sakal and his razors to me this instant." In the course of a few minutes the Barber stood before him.

"Why do you refuse to shave this man's companion?" asked the Caliph, "Was not that your agreement?"

Ali kissed the ground before the throne, and answered, "It is true, O Caliph, that such was our agreement, but whoever made a companion of a donkey before? Or whoever thought of shaving one?"

"You may say right," answered the Caliph, "but whoever thought of insisting that a packsaddle should be included in a load of wood? No, no! It is the Woodcutter's turn now. Shave the donkey immediately, or lose your head."

The donkey was brought in, and the Barber, filled with mortification, was obliged to prepare a great quantity of soapsuds, and to lather the beast from head to feet. He then had to shave it in the presence of the Caliph and his court, whilst all who looked on jeered and laughed at him.

As for the poor Woodcutter, as soon as his donkey was shaved, the Caliph presented him with a purse filled with gold pieces, and the man returned to his family rejoicing.

The Parrot
and the Parson

🌷🌷🌷

THERE WAS ONCE a Banker who taught his Parrot the speech of men. The Parrot made such progress that he was soon able to take part in any conversation, and he astonished everyone by his intelligence.

One day a Parson passed by the Parrot as he sat in his cage.

"My respects to Your Reverence," said the Parrot.

The Parson looked all around him; he looked down at his feet; he looked up into the trees; but no one could he see who might have spoken to him. He could not make it out; he thought it must have been a ghost.

Then the Parrot spoke again. "It was I who greeted you," said he. The Parrot's cage was close to the Parson's ear, and now at length the Parson saw him. The Parrot went on—

"O reverend sir, you teach men how to get free from the chains of their sins. May it please you to tell me how to escape from this cage?"

This was a practical question, but the Parson's advice was not usually asked on practical matters. He did not know what to say.

"I fear I can be of no use to you," said he, "but I will consult my Lawyer."

The Parson went to see his Lawyer, and paid him a certain sum in order to ask his advice. (He might have bought the Parrot, cage and all, for half the sum; but, as I have said, he was not a practical man.) When he told the Lawyer what business he came about, the Lawyer said nothing at all, but fell down in a faint.

"What can I have said to make him faint?" the Parson thought. "Perhaps it is the hot weather."

He poured water over the Lawyer's face, and by-and-by the Lawyer came to.

The Parson was much distressed at having thrown away his money; but he knew it would be of no use asking his Lawyer to give any of it back, so he did not try. He went back to the Parrot and said—

"Dearly beloved Bird, I much regret having no information to give you which may be of use. The fact is, no sooner did I put your question to my worthy Lawyer, than he fell down in a dead faint."

"Oh," said the Parrot, "many thanks, Parson."

The Parson went away to the parish meeting. When he had gone, the Parrot stretched himself out on the bottom of his cage, and shut his eyes, and cocked his feet up in the air.

By-and-by the Banker came in, and saw his Parrot lying on his back, with his feet pointing to the sky.

"Poor Poll," said he, "you're dead, my pretty Poll."

He opened the door of the cage, and took out the bird, and laid him on the ground. Immediately the Parrot opened his wings and flew away.

The Lost Camel

❧❧❧

A DERVISH was journeying alone in the desert, when two Merchants suddenly met him. "You have lost a camel," said he to the Merchants.

"Indeed we have," they replied.

"Was he not blind in his right eye, and lame in his left leg?" said the Dervish.

"He was," replied the Merchants.

"Had he lost a front tooth?" said the Dervish.

"He had," rejoined the Merchants.

"And was he not loaded with honey on one side, and wheat on the other?"

"Most certainly he was," they replied "and you have seen him so lately, and marked him so particularly, you can, in all probability, conduct us to him."

"My friends," said the Dervish, "I have never seen your camel, nor ever heard of him but from yourselves."

"A pretty story, truly!" said the Merchants. "But where are the jewels which formed a part of his cargo?"

"I have neither seen your camel nor your jewels," repeated the Dervish.

On this they seized him, and hurried him before the Cadi, or Judge, where, on the strictest search, nothing could be found upon him, nor could any evidence be offered to convict him, either of falsehood or of theft. They were then about to proceed against him as a sorcerer, when the Dervish, with great calmness, thus addressed the court: "I have been much amused with your surprise, and own that there has been some ground for your suspicions; but I have lived long, and alone; and I can find ample scope for observation, even in a desert. I knew that I had crossed the track of a camel that had strayed from its owner, because I saw no mark of any human footsteps on the same route; I knew that the animal was blind of one eye, because it had cropped the herbage only on one side of the path; and I perceived that it was lame of one leg from the faint impression that one of its feet had produced upon the sand; I concluded that the animal had lost one tooth, because wherever it had grazed, a small tuft of grass was left uninjured, in the center of its bite. As to that which formed the burden of the beast, the busy ants informed me that it was wheat on the one side, and the clustering flies, that it was honey on the other."

Jupiter and the Horse

❧❧❧

"FATHER OF MAN AND BEAST," said the Horse, approaching the throne of Jupiter, "it is said that I am one of the noblest creatures with which you have adorned the world, and my vanity tells me to believe it. But do you not think it would still be possible to improve my form?"

"And how do you propose to improve it? Speak, for I am open to suggestions," returned Jupiter, smiling graciously.

"Perhaps," returned the Horse, "I might have more speed if my legs were longer and more slender; a long swanlike neck would add to my beauty; a broader chest would increase my strength; and since you have destined me to carry upon my back your favorite, man, it might be well if the saddle, which my kind rider provides me with, should once and for all be made part of my body."

"Excellent," replied Jupiter. "Wait a moment!" And then, with a solemn air, he spoke the Word of Creation. The dust received the breath of life, matter took on its appointed form; and suddenly there stood before the throne the ungainly Camel. The Horse saw, shrank back, and shuddered in disgust and fear.

"Here," said Jupiter, "are longer and more slender legs; here is a long swanlike neck, a broader chest, a ready-made saddle. Is this the form you wish in place of your own?"

The Horse continued to shudder in silence.

"Go," concluded Jupiter, "and this time the warning shall be sufficient without further punishment. But in order to remind you from time to time of the folly of your audacity, this new creation shall continue to exist." Then, casting a sustaining glance upon the Camel, he added, "And no Horse shall ever look upon the Camel without fear and trembling."

How the Fog Came

🌷🌷🌷

THERE WAS A MOUNTAIN SPIRIT, which stole corpses from their graves and ate them when it came home. And a Man, wishing to see who did this thing, let himself be buried alive. The Spirit came, and saw the new grave, and dug up the body, and carried it off.

The Man had stuck a flat stone in under his coat, in case the Spirit should try to stab him.

On the way, he caught hold of all the willow twigs whenever they passed any bushes, and made himself as heavy as he could, so that the Spirit was forced to put forth all its strength.

At last the Spirit reached its house, and flung down the body on the floor. And then, being weary, it lay down to sleep, while its wife went out to gather wood for the cooking.

"Father, Father, he is opening his eyes," cried the children, when the Dead Man suddenly looked up.

"Nonsense, Children, it is a dead body, which I have dropped many times among the twigs on the way," said the Father.

But the Man rose up, and killed the Mountain Spirit and its children, and fled away as fast as he could. The Mountain Spirit's wife saw him, and mistook him for her husband.

"Where are you going?" she cried.

The Man did not answer, but fled on. And the Woman, thinking something must be wrong, ran after him.

And as he was running over level ground, he cried:

"Rise up, hills!

And at once many hills rose up.

Then the Mountain Spirit's wife lagged behind, having to climb up so many hills.

The Man saw a little stream, and sprang across.

"Flow over your banks!" he cried to the stream. And now it was impossible for her to get across.

"How did you get across?" cried the Woman.

"I drank up the water. Do you likewise."

And the Woman began gulping it down.

Then the Man turned around towards her, and said: "Look at the hem of your tunic; it is hanging down."

And when she bent down to look, her belly burst.

And as she burst, a steam rose up out of her, and turned to fog, which still floats about to this day among the hills.

The Tiger and the Frog

❦❦❦

IT IS BUT SELDOM tigers leave their homes in the warm jungles or frogs their homes in the swamp. However, it has happened, and here follows a story of a Tiger and a Frog who both wandered very far from their homes. The home of the Tiger was in Nepal, and that of the Frog in Tibet. Thirst had driven the Tiger on a long journey in quest of water. As for the Frog, he was curious, that was all.

In a certain place where the two countries border on one another, the Tiger had found a pool, and he had a long drink, for he was very thirsty. The Frog happened to be hopping near by and saw the Tiger drinking, and the Tiger, looking up, saw the Frog. The curiosity of the Frog led him to hop to the pool, and he, too, had a drink. After he swallowed the water, he felt a tickling in his throat.

"Hullo!" said the Tiger. "Who are you?"

"I am a frog," replied the Frog, and he asked the Tiger who he was.

The Tiger said, "I am a tiger."

The Frog had heard tell of tigers, and he anxiously inquired of the Tiger what he ate.

"Frogs," replied the Tiger, promptly opening his large jaws and showing a double row of grinders. "Frogs are most succulent. Yes, I eat frogs."

On hearing this the Frog felt alarmed and wished he had remained at home.

However, the Tiger could have caught him in one fell swoop if he attempted to hop away, so he said quickly, "That is strange, because I eat tigers."

On hearing this the Tiger roared with laughter till his great sides shook.

"If," continued the Frog, "you truly eat frogs, prove it to me. Return what you have eaten, because I find it difficult to believe."

"Certainly," said the Tiger, "if you will do the same, for your story is even more difficult to believe."

"I will," said the Frog, who knew that it was the Tiger's hair that was tickling in his throat. "Nothing could be easier than to prove the truth of what I have told you."

The Tiger thereupon brought up some grass, but the Frog with one cough brought up the Tiger's hair.

"There you are," said the Frog. But the Tiger

didn't wait to hear any more. He turned tail and bolted and left the Frog to compliment himself on the success of his trick.

Being a wise Frog, he hopped back as quickly as he knew how to his homeland swamp to boast to his friends of how he had outwitted a Tiger and saved his own skin.

As for the Tiger, he ran quicker than he had ever run before in his life. He was still running when a Jackal crossed his path.

"Hi, Tiger!" called the Jackal. "What's your hurry? You run as if a devil was after you."

"A devil," panted the Tiger, slowing down. "Worse than that. Over yonder in Tibet I met a Frog who eats tigers."

"A Frog who eats tigers!" exclaimed the Jackal. "That is absurd. Come, tie your whiskers to mine, and together we will go back and have a look at the curious monster."

"No, no," said the Tiger, quaking. But the Jackal said, "Tiger, what a coward you are," and insisted they should turn back.

So the Tiger and the Jackal knitted their whiskers together and went back. After awhile they came to the swamp where the Frog lived. The Frog was squatting on a stone sunning himself when the Tiger and the Jackal made their appearance.

"Ho," said the Frog, who had told his story so often that he really believed he could eat a tiger. "Ho, so I see you have come back to be eaten, Tiger."

"There! What did I tell you?" said the Tiger to the Jackal. And he turned back and fled, dragging the poor Jackal after him. The Tiger ran and ran, and the Jackal, who could not run so fast, got more and more breathless, until all the breath left his body, and he died.

The Tiger, feeling the dead weight of the Jackal, thought, "Ah, he is trying to drag me back. He is in league with the Frog."

"Untie my whiskers," commanded the Tiger. There was no answer.

"Untie my whiskers." Still no answer.

"Take that," said the Tiger, half turning, and he gave the Jackal a clout on the ear.

The Jackal, who was now rigid, rocked stiffly.

"Hump!" said the Tiger. "So you thought you would take me to the Frog to be eaten," and he gave the Jackal another good whack and proceeded to lecture him.

"Yes," went on the Tiger. "You thought you could bind me fast, tying your whiskers to mine, so that I would stand there to be eaten by the Frog, you treacherous beast. Take *that*—and *that*," said the Tiger and he gave the Jackal a few more clouts.

The Jackal rocked and fell sideways.

"You wanted me to suffer the indignity of being eaten by a frog," and the Tiger wrenched his whiskers free from the Jackal's.

The Jackal lay stiff and stark on the road. The Tiger noticed an unpleasant odor. "The devil's entered into him, and he pretends to be asleep," thought the Tiger, whose nerves were on edge.

Freed from the Jackal, he ran faster yet. Presently he met a Tortoise. The Tortoise called: "What makes you run so fast, Tiger?" The Tiger stopped to tell him.

"I've left a Jackal over there," said he, "who

has a devil in him. A treacherous rascal who tried to get me devoured by a frog."

"Where?" inquired the Tortoise. "Let me have a look at him."

"Not I," said the Tiger, and he fell to the ground in a dead faint.

The Tortoise crawled to where the poor Jackal lay and perceived that the Jackal was dead. "What a fool of a tiger," thought the Tortoise, and he gave the Jackal a decent burial.

"A Tiger who is afraid of a dead Jackal and a harmless Frog. A fine lord of beasts—let him stay as he is in a faint," and the Tortoise gave a sniff and slid into the water.

The Wise Old Shepherd

✿✿✿

ONCE UPON A TIME, a Snake went out of his hole to take an airing. He crawled about, greatly enjoying the scenery and the fresh whiff of the breeze, when he saw an open door, and he went in. Now this door was the door of the palace of the King, and inside was the King himself, with all his Courtiers.

Imagine their horror at seeing a huge Snake crawling in at the door. They all ran away except the King, who felt that his rank forbade him to be a coward, and the King's son. The King called out for somebody to come and kill the Snake. None of the Courtiers would do as the King ordered, but the young Prince obeyed his father, and killed the Snake with his stick.

After a while the Snake's wife became anxious,

and set out in search of her husband. She, too, saw the open door of the palace, and in she went.

O horror! There on the floor lay the body of her husband, all covered with blood, and quite dead. No one saw the Snake's wife crawl in; she inquired from an ant what had happened, and when she found that the young Prince had killed her husband, she made a vow, that as he had made her a widow, so she would make his wife a widow.

That night, while all the world was asleep, the Snake's wife crept into the Prince's bedroom, and coiled around his neck. The Prince slept on, and when he awoke in the morning, he was surprised to find his neck encircled with the coils of a snake. He was afraid to stir, so there he remained, until the Princess, his wife, became anxious, and went to see what was the matter. When she entered his room, and saw him in this plight, she gave a loud shriek, and ran off to tell the King.

"Call the Archers," said the King. The Archers came, and the King told them to go into the Prince's room, and shoot the Snake that was coiled about his son's neck. They were so clever, that they could easily do this without hurting the Prince at all.

In came the Archers in a row, fitted the arrows

to the bows, the bows were raised and ready to shoot, when, on a sudden, from the Snake there issued a voice, which spoke as follows:—

"O Archers! Wait, and hear me before you shoot. It is not fair to carry out the sentence before you have heard the case. Is not this your law, 'An eye for an eye, and a tooth for a tooth'? Is it not so, O King?"

"Yes," replied the King, "that is our law."

"Then," said the Snake's wife, "I plead the law. Your son has made me a widow, so it is fair and right that I should make his wife a widow."

"That *sounds* right enough," said the King, "but right and law are not always the same thing. We had better ask somebody who knows."

They asked all the Judges, but none of them could tell the law of the matter. They shook their heads, and said they would read all their law-books, and see whether anything of the sort had ever happened before, and if so, how it had been decided. The upshot of it all was, that not a judge would give any opinion; so the King sent Messengers all over the countryside, to see if they could find somebody somewhere who knew something.

One of these messengers found a party of five Shepherds, who were sitting upon a hill and trying to decide a quarrel of their own. They gave their opinions so freely, and in language so very strong, that the King's Messenger said to himself, "Here are the men for us. Here are five men, each with an opinion of his own, and all different." Posthaste he scurried back to the King, and told him he had found at last someone ready to judge the knotty point.

So the King and the Queen, and the Prince and the Princess, and all the Courtiers got on horseback, and away they galloped to the hill whereupon the five Shepherds were sitting, and the Snake's wife, too, went with them, coiled round the neck of the Prince.

When they got to the Shepherds' hill, the Shepherds were dreadfully frightened. But the King and his Court got off their horses, and said good-day in the most polite way. So the Shepherds felt their minds set at ease again. Then the King said:

"Worthy Shepherds, we have a question to put to you, which not all the Judges in all the courts of my city have been able to solve. Here is my son, and here, as you see, is a Snake coiled round his neck. Now, the husband of this Snake came creeping into my palace hall, and my son the Prince killed him; so this Snake, who is the wife of the other, says that as my son has made her a widow, so she has a right to widow my son's wife. What do you think about it?"

The first Shepherd said, "I think she is quite right, my lord King. If anyone made my wife a widow, I would pretty soon do the same to him."

This was brave language, and the other Shepherds shook their heads and looked fierce. But the King was puzzled, and could not quite understand it. You see, in the first place, if the man's wife were a widow, the man would be dead; and then it is hard to see how he could do anything. So to make sure, the King asked the second Shepherd whether that was his opinion, too.

"Yes," said the second Shepherd. "Now the Prince has killed the Snake, the Snake has a right to kill the Prince, if he can."

But that was not of much use either, as the

Snake was as dead as a doornail. So the King passed on to the third.

"I agree with the others," said the third Shepherd, "because, you see, a prince is a prince, but then a snake is a snake."

That was quite true, they all admitted; but it did not seem to help the matter much. Then the King asked the fourth Shepherd to say what he thought.

The fourth Shepherd said, "An eye for an eye, and a tooth for a tooth; so I think a widow should be a widow, if she doesn't marry again."

By this time the poor King was so puzzled that he hardly knew whether he stood on his head or his heels. But there was still the fifth Shepherd left, the oldest and the wisest of them all; and the fifth Shepherd said:

"O King, I should like to ask two questions."

"Ask twenty, if you like," said the King. He did not promise to answer them, so he could afford to be generous.

"First, I ask the Princess how many sons she has?"

"Four," said the Princess.

"And how many sons has Mistress Snake here?"

"Seven," said the Snake.

"Then," said the old Shepherd, "it will be quite

fair for Mistress Snake to kill His Highness the
Prince, when Her Highness the Princess has had
three sons more."

"I never thought of that," said the Snake's
wife. "Good-bye, King, and all you good people.
Send a message when the Princess has had three
more sons, and you may count upon me—I will
not fail you." So saying, she uncoiled from the
Prince's neck and slid away among the grass.

The King and the Prince and everybody shook
hands with the wise old Shepherd, and went home
again. And as the Princess never had any more
sons at all, she and the Prince lived happily for
many years; and if they are not dead they are living still.

The Wily Tortoise

A FOWLER WAS bird-catching in the jungle, and snared a wild Goose. As he was carrying home his goose, he sat down by the pond. In this pond lived a Tortoise, and the Tortoise put up his nose out of the pond to sniff the air. He saw the Fowler and the Goose, and being a very innocent tortoise, he feared no harm, but began to waddle towards him.

"Take care, friend!" said the Goose. "This Fowler has caught me, and he will catch you!"

The Tortoise waddled into the water again. "Many thanks, friend," said he. "One good turn deserves another."

So saying, he dived down into the pond, and brought up a ruby.

"Here, Mr. Fowler," said he, "take this ruby, and let my friend the Goose go."

The Fowler took the ruby, but he was very greedy, so he said: "If you will bring me a pair like this, I will let the Goose go."

The Tortoise dived down, and brought up another ruby. Then the Fowler let go the Goose and the Goose flew away. The Fowler said to the Tortoise, "Now hand over that ruby."

The Tortoise said, "Forgive me, but I think I have made a mistake, and brought up the wrong ruby. Let me see the first, and if it does not match, I will try again."

The Fowler gave back the first ruby. The Tortoise looked at it and said, "Just as I thought; the two do not match."

Down he dived into the pond.

The Fowler waited a good long time, but nothing was seen of the Tortoise. As you have guessed, when the Tortoise found himself safe at the bottom of the pond, he stayed there.

The Fowler tore his hair, and went home, wishing he had not been so greedy.

How the Coyote Stole Fire for the Klamaths

❦❦❦

In the beginning the Klamaths had no fire. The only fire in the world was guarded by two very bad-hearted old Devil-Women, not the same as those who kept the salmon from coming upstream; two different ones. They lived in their great lodges, which are now the white-topped twin mountain. The fire was inside the mountain.

Again the Coyote came to the Man and said: "Why do you not get some fire for yourself and your children?"

The Man said, "I cannot; the Devil-Women have it."

Then the Coyote said, "I will get it for you, because you were good to me; wait, I shall be back."

The Coyote went to all the animals and told them they must do as he said, and help him steal fire from the witches. Then he put them in a long line, from the Fire Mountain to the home of the Klamaths, each one about as far from the next as he could make a good run. The swiftest and strongest he placed nearest the Devil-Women's lodges.

The Eagle was first, just a little way off; then, a long way down the mountain, was the Cougar; then the Bear; then the Elk and Deer; then, across the open prairie, the Antelope, the swiftest animal; then the Rabbit, with his long bushy white tail; and all the animals down to the Squirrel, and last of all the Frog. The Frog was not then so small as he is now: he was a large animal and could give great leaps; but he was the slowest. He was put at the edge of the river, where the Klamaths lived.

The Coyote, when he had got all the animals ready, came for the Man, and together they went to the fire lodges of the old women. When they were there, the Coyote made the Man wound him a little bit in the skin of one leg, not much; and the Man cut himself, too, and smeared plenty of blood over the Coyote.

Then the Coyote went limping on three legs to the lodge, and crept in, whining and crying.

"What is the matter, Italapas?" said the Devil-Women, cracking their great teeth together as cranes clash their bills, only louder.

"The Man had tried to kill me," said the Coyote, and showed his wounds. "But I have bitten him so he will die. Smell; some of this blood is his."

Then the old Women sniffed the blood and gnashed their teeth more than ever, and laughed so the mountain shook, and down in the mountain you could hear the rumble of their laughter.

"Lie down by the sacred fire," said they to the Coyote.

He lay down and commenced to lick his leg. After a time he pretended to fall asleep, and stretched himself out before the fire and snored.

Presently the Devil-Women dropped their chins on their breasts and dozed. Then, like the dart of a salmon, the Coyote seized a brand and fled. The

hags followed after him, screaming and gnashing their teeth. They were nearly on him, when he handed the brand to the Eagle.

Away flew the great bird, his wings hitting the air like a tempest in the pines. But the old Women followed fast and never grew tired. The Eagle was glad to give the fire to the Cougar; so it went down the line, the Devil-Women just missing it each time, and shrieking with anger as they pursued each new fire-bearer. They were so close to the Rabbit that, just as he gave it to the Bat, one old Woman siezed his tail and pulled it off; that is why Rabbits are stump-tailed.

The Bat took the fire; he could not fly very fast, but always, just as the old Women thought they had him, he would dodge. They could not touch him, for he dodged this way and that, and brought the fire safe to the Squirrel. When the fire got to the Squirrel, it was much smaller than it had been, but it had been fanned into a blaze, and in carrying it he scorched his back; so that his tail was drawn clear over his back, and the brown is on his fur to this day.

At last it came to the Frog; but he, knowing he could not outrun the old Women, swallowed the fire and jumped into the river.

Then, with yells of rage, the Devil-Women gave up the chase and went back to their lodges.

Their fire went out, and there they stand today, cold and white.

When they had gone, the Frog came up and spit the fire out into a log; which is why it can be got by twirling one stick of wood very fast on another. The fire had burned the Frog inside so badly that he shrank to the little fellow he is now, and his eyes nearly popped out of his head with pain.

The Cat
and the Sparrows

THERE WAS ONCE a pair of Sparrows that lived in a tree. They used to hop about all over the place, picking up seeds or anything they could find to eat. One day, when they came back with their pickings, the Cock had found some rice, and the Hen a few lentils. They put it all in an earthen pot, and then the Hen proceeded to cook their dinner. When it was cooked they divided it into two equal parts.

The Cock was rather greedy, so he would not wait while his wife put out the fire and got ready to join in the meal. No! he gobbled up his share at once, before she could begin.

When at last the poor Hen came up, her greedy mate would not let her rest even then. "Go and get me a drink of water," said he quite rudely.

She was a very kind wife, so without taking

any notice of his rudeness, off she went for the water.

While she was gone the Cock-Sparrow's eyes fell on his wife's share of the dinner. "Ah," thought he, "how I should like another bit! Well, why shouldn't I have it? A man does all the work, and women don't want much to eat at any time." So without any more ado, he just set to, and gobbled up his wife's share.

Back came the Hen-Sparrow with a drink of water for her husband. When he had drunk it up (and I am afraid he forgot to say thank you), she turned to look for her dinner. Lo and behold! there was none. What could have become of it? As she was wondering, she happened to look at her husband; he looked so guilty that there could be no manner of doubt where her dinner was.

"You greedy bird," said she, "why have you eaten my dinner?"

"I haven't touched your dinner," said the Cock angrily.

"I'm sure you have," said she, "or you would not look so guilty. Why you are actually blushing." And so indeed he was; the tip of his beak was quite red.

However, he still denied it, and grew angrier and angrier, as people do when they know they are in the wrong. They had a terrible quarrel. At

last the Hen-Sparrow said, "Well, I know a way
to find out whether you are telling lies or not. You
come along with me." And she made him go with
her to the well.

Across the top of the well she stretched a piece
of string, and she sat on the middle of the string,
and began to chirp, "If I am telling lies, I pray
I may fall in." But though she sat there a long
time, chirping away, she did not fall in.

Then came the Cock-Sparrow's turn. He
perched on the string and begin to chirrup, "If
I am telling lies, may I fall into the well." But
hardly had he got the words out of his mouth,
when—splash! down he went.

Then the Hen was very sorry that she had proposed this plan; she began to weep and cheep,
and said:

"Alas, alas, why didn't I leave it alone? What
does it matter if he eats my dinner, so long as I
have my dear husband? Now I have killed him
by my folly."

Just at that moment up came a Cat.

"What's the matter?" said the Cat.

"Cheep, cheep, cheep," went the Hen-Sparrow.
"My husband has fallen into the well, and I don't
know how to get him out."

"If I get him out," said the Cat, "will you let
me eat him?"

"Of course you may," said the Hen-Sparrow.

So the Cat climbed down, and pulled out the Cock-Sparrow. When she had brought him to the edge of the well, said she, "Now I'm going to eat him as you promised."

"Oh, all right," said the Hen. "But stop a minute, your mouth is dirty. I am sure you have been eating mice. Now haven't you?"

"Why, yes," said the Cat, "so I have."

"Well," said the Hen-Sparrow, "you must get yourself clean. We birds are clean creatures, and you must positively wash your mouth before you begin."

Away went the Cat, and washed her mouth clean, and came back again.

The Hen-Sparrow looked at her carefully. "You have not washed your whiskers;" said she, "they are still dirty."

The Cat went obediently and washed her whiskers.

Meanwhile the Cock-Sparrow had been sitting on the edge of the well in the sun, and by this time his feathers were quite dry.

So his Hen chirped to him, "Now, dear, you can fly, let's be off." And off they flew together.

And the Cat was left licking her chops and wishing she had not been so foolish as to listen to the Hen-Sparrow.

The Race

ONCE OLD MAN was traveling around, when he heard some very queer singing. He had never heard anything like this before, and looked all around to see who it was.

At last he saw it was the cottontail rabbits, singing and making medicine. They had built a fire, and got a lot of hot ashes, and they would lie down in these ashes and sing while one covered them up. They would stay there only a short time though, for the ashes were very hot.

"Little Brothers," said Old Man, "that is very wonderful, how you lie in these hot ashes and coals without burning. I wish you would teach me how to do it."

"Come on, Old Man," said the Rabbits, "we will show you how to do it. You must sing our song, and only stay in the ashes a short time."

So the Old Man began to sing, and he lay down, and they covered him with coals and ashes, and they did not burn him at all.

"That is very nice," he said. "You have powerful medicine. Now I want to know it all, so you lie down and let me cover you up."

So the rabbits all lay down in the ashes, and Old Man covered them up, and then he put the whole fire over them. One old Rabbit got out, and Old Man was about to put her back when she said, "Pity me, my children are about to be born."

"All right," replied Old Man. "I will let you go, so there will be some more rabbits; but I will roast these nicely and have a feast." And he put more wood on the fire. When the rabbits were cooked, he cut some red willow brush, and laid them on it to cool. The grease soaked into these branches, so, even today if you hold red willow over a fire, you will see the grease on the bark. You can see, too, that ever since, the rabbits have a burnt place on their backs, where the one that got away was singed.

Old Man sat down, and was waiting for the rabbits to cool a little, when a Coyote came along, limping very badly.

"Pity me, Old Man," he said, "you have lots of cooked rabbits; give me one of them."

"Go away," exclaimed Old Man. "If you are too lazy to catch your food, I will not help you."

"My leg is broken," said the Coyote. "I can't catch anything, and I'm starving. Just give me half a rabbit."

"I don't care if you die," replied Old Man. "I

worked hard to cook all these rabbits, and I will
not give any away. But I will tell you what to do.
We will run a race to that butte, way out there,
and if you beat me you can have a rabbit."

"All right," said the Coyote. So they started.
Old Man ran very fast, and the Coyote limped
along behind, but close to him, until they got near
to the butte. Then the Coyote turned round and
ran back very fast, for he was not lame at all.

It took Old Man a long time to go back, and
just before he got to the fire, the Coyote swallowed
the last rabbit, and trotted off over the prairie.

Why the Possum's Tail Is Bare

❧❧❧

Possum used to have a long, bushy tail and he was so proud of it that he combed it out every morning and sang about it at the dance. Now Rabbit had had no tail since Bear pulled it off because he was jealous. Therefore he planned to play a trick on Possum.

The animals called a great council. They planned to have a dance. It was Rabbit's business to send out the news. One day as he was passing Possum's house, he stopped to talk.

"Are you going to the council?" he asked.

"Yes, if I can have a special seat," said Possum. "I have such a handsome tail, I ought to sit where everyone can see me."

Rabbit said, "I will see that you have a special seat. And I will send someone to comb your tail for the dance." Possum was very much pleased.

Rabbit at once went to Cricket, who is an expert hair cutter; that is why the Indians call him the barber. He told Cricket to go the next morning and comb Possum's tail for the dance. He told Cricket *just what to do.*

In the morning, Cricket went to Possum's house. Possum stretched himself out on the floor and went to sleep, while Cricket combed out his tail and wrapped a red string around it to keep it smooth until night. But all the time, as he wound the string around, he was snipping off the hair closely. Possum did not know it.

When it was night, Possum went to the council and took his special seat. When it was his turn to dance. he loosened the red string from his tail and stepped into the middle of the lodge.

The Drummers began to beat the drum. Possum began to sing, "See my beautiful tail."

Every man shouted and Possum danced around the circle again, singing, "See what a fine color it has." They all shouted again, and Possum went on dancing, as he sang, "See how it sweeps the ground."

Then the animals all shouted so that Possum wondered what it meant. He looked around. Every man was laughing at him. Then he looked down at his beautiful tail. It was as bare as a lizard's tail. There was not a hair on it.

He was so astonished and ashamed that he could not say a word. He rolled over on the ground and grinned, just as he does today when taken by surprise.

The Man Who Ate His Wives

❦❦❦

AMONG THE ESKIMO it is told that once there was a man who was wont to eat his wives. He managed it this way. He fattened them up, giving them nothing but salmon to eat, and nothing at all to drink. When they were so fat they couldn't move, he harpooned them.

Once when he had just lost his wife in the usual way, he took to wife the sister of many brothers, and her name was Misána. And after having taken her to be his wife, he began fattening her up as he had his other wives.

One day the man went out in his kayak. And Misána had grown so fat that she could hardly move, but somehow she managed with difficulty to tumble from the bench to the floor. She crawled to the entrance, dropped down into the passageway, and began licking the snow which had drifted in. She licked and licked at it, and at last she began to feel herself lighter, and lighter. She was able to move again. And in this way she afterwards went out and licked up snow whenever her husband was out in his Kayak, and at last she was once more quite able to move about.

One day when her husband was out in his kayak as usual, she took her breeches and tunic, and stuffed them until they looked like a real human being, and then she said to them:

"When my husband comes and tells you to come out, answer him with these words: 'I cannot move because I am grown so fat.' And when he then comes in and harpoons you, remember then to shriek as if in pain."

And after she had said these words, she began digging a hole at the back of the house, and when it was big enough, she crept in.

No sooner had Misána crept into her hole and concealed herself than her husband came in. He called out:

"Bring up the birds I have caught."

But the dummy answered:

"I can no longer move, because I am grown so fat."

Now the dummy was sitting behind the lamp. And the husband coming in, harpooned that dummy wife with his great bird-spear. And the

thing shrieked as if with pain and fell down. But
when the husband looked closer, there was no
blood to be seen, nothing but some stuffed out-
clothes. And where was his wife?

He began to search for her, and as soon as he
had gone out, she crept forth from her hiding
place, and took to flight. And while she was thus
making her escape, her husband came after her,
and seeing that he came nearer and nearer, at last
she said:

"My amulet is a piece of wood." And she said
some magic words. Hardly had she said these
words, when she was changed into a piece of
wood, and her husband could not find her.

He looked about as hard as he could, but could
see nothing beyond a piece of wood anywhere.
And he stabbed at that once or twice with his
knife, but Misána felt no more than a little sting-
ing pain. Then he went back to fetch his ax, and
then, as soon as he was out of sight, Misána
changed back into a woman again and fled away
to her brothers.

When she came to their house, she hid herself
behind the skin hangings. She told her brothers
all that happened. No sooner than she finished
telling them about her husband when her husband was heard approaching. He was weeping
because he had lost his wife.

He stayed with them, and in the evening, the brothers began singing songs in mockery of him, and turning towards him, they said:

"Men say that you eat your wives."

"Who has said that?" asked the man.

"Misána has said that," said the brothers.

"I said it, and I ran away because you tried to kill me," said she from behind the hangings.

And then Misána's many brothers fell upon the man and held him fast that their sister might kill him; she took her knife, but each time she tried to strike, the knife only grazed his skin, for her fingers lost their power.

And she was still standing there trying in vain to stab him, when they saw that he was already dead.

Here ends the story.

The Giant
and the Dwarf

THERE CAME from far-off lands a strong man, a Giant, who had nowhere met his match, and he challenged anyone in the whole kingdom to wrestle with him. The King gathered his people together, but, to his amazement, could not for a long time find anybody ready to face the Giant, till, at last, there came forth a weak insignificant-looking Dwarf, who offered to wrestle with the Giant.

Looking down at the Dwarf, the Giant sniffed at the idea of wrestling with a Dwarf and such an insignificant-looking one at that. He turned away for he did not believe that the Dwarf was serious. But the Dwarf insisted that he was serious and that he meant to wrestle with the Giant. He only asked that the Giant's strength should be put to the proof before the struggle began.

The Giant angrily seized a stone, and clasping it in his fingers, squeezed until he got some moisture out of it.

So the Dwarf picked up a stone and cleverly replaced it with a sponge which looked like the stone, and he squeezed the sponge until a stream of water poured out.

The Giant then picked up another stone and threw it so violently on the ground that it became dust.

The Dwarf then picked up a stone which he cunningly hid and then he threw on the ground a handful of flour, to the great astonishment of the Giant.

Stretching forth his hand to the Dwarf, the Giant said: "You must come home with me. I never expected to find so much strength in such a small man. I will not wrestle with you; but give me your hand in token of friendship and brotherhood."

The Dwarf agreed to go home with the Giant but he did not give the Giant his hand. The Giant asked the Dwarf why he would not shake his hand in a brotherly manner.

The Dwarf replied: "I am unable to moderate the force of my pressure, and more than one man has already died from the fearful force of my hand."

Then the new brothers set out together. On their way to the Giant's house, they came to a stream which had to be forded. The Dwarf feared he would be carried away by the current. He told the Giant that he was suffering from a stomach-ache and did not therefore wish to go into the cold water, so he asked the Giant to carry him over.

In the midst of the stream, the Giant, with the Dwarf on his shoulders, suddenly stopped and said: "I have heard that strong people are heavy, but I do not feel you on my shoulders. Tell me how this is."

"Since we have become brothers," replied the Dwarf, "I have no right to press with all my

weight upon you, and did I not support myself by holding on to the sky with one hand, you could never carry me."

But the Giant, wishing to test his strength, asked the Dwarf to drop his hand for a moment, whereupon the Dwarf took from his pocket two nails, and stuck the sharp points of them in the shoulders of the Giant.

The Giant could not endure the pain, and immediately begged the Dwarf, "Please lighten my load at once—grab hold of the sky with one hand again."

To please the Giant, the Dwarf said he would. And then the Giant finished carrying the Dwarf across the stream.

When they reached the other side, the two new friends soon came to the Giant's house. The Giant wished to give a special dinner to the Dwarf and he proposed that they should share in the work of getting it ready. One of them should take the bread out of the oven, while the other should get the wine from the cellar.

The Dwarf saw in the oven an immense loaf which he could never have lifted, so he chose to go down to the cellar for the wine. But when he went down to the cellar, he found he was unable to lift the weights on the tops of the jars, so, thinking that by this time the Giant would have

taken the loaf out of the oven, he called out: "Shall
I bring up all the jars?"

The Giant, alarmed, lest the Dwarf should spoil
his whole year's stock of wine by digging the jars
out of the ground where they were buried, rushed
down into the cellar, and the Dwarf went upstairs.

But great was the astonishment of the Dwarf
when he found that the bread was still in the oven,
and that he must take it out, willy-nilly. He suc-
ceeded with difficulty in dragging a loaf to the
edge of the oven, but then he fell with the hot
bread on top of him, and being unable to free himself, was almost smothered.

Just then the Giant came in, and asked what
had happened. The Dwarf replied: "As I told you
this morning, I am suffering from a stomachache,
and, in order to soothe the pain, I applied the hot
loaf as a plaster."

Then the Giant went over to the Dwarf and
said: "Poor fellow! How do you feel now, after
your plaster?"

"Better, thank you," replied the Dwarf. "I feel
so much better that you can take off the loaf."

The Giant lifted the loaf, and the two men
then sat down to dinner. Suddenly the Giant
sneezed so hard that the Dwarf was blown up to
the roof, and he seized a beam, so that he should
not fall down again.

The Giant looked up with astonishment, and asked:

"What does that mean? What are you doing up there?"

The Dwarf angrily replied: "If you do such a vulgar thing again I shall pull this beam out and break it over your stupid head."

The Giant apologized, and promised that he would never sneeze again during dinnertime; then he brought a ladder and placed it beneath the Dwarf. The Dwarf let go of the beam and came down.

The Giant and the Dwarf finished their dinner. And as far as I know the Giant never sneezed again when he and the Dwarf were eating.

The Monkey
and the Heron

❦❦❦

A MONKEY AND A HERON once struck up a close friendship, and thought it would be amusing to take a journey together. So they set out, the Monkey hopping and leaping along, while the Heron strutted on his long legs beside him. The Monkey continually stopped to pick berries and to play with this, that, or the other, on the road, and the Heron had to urge him not to dawdle. Neither of them knew where they were making for, and when the Monkey asked the Heron why they need hurry, the Heron replied, "To get somewhere before dark."

"If that's all," said the Monkey, "let me be. I'm somewhere at the present moment, and have always been somewhere for as long as I can remember."

However, when it did get dark the Monkey

shivered, his teeth chattered, and he begged the Heron to find a place to sleep. The Heron found a tree growing in the middle of a swamp, and he told the Monkey to get on his back, and he would wade on his long legs through the swamp, and they would sleep safely in the branches.

"I could not have found a better place," said the Heron. "No dangerous beast can get at us here, for the ground is swampy all around."

The Monkey clambered to a topmost branch, and the Heron settled himself on a lower one. The Heron, knowing what a fidgety fellow the Monkey was, and feeling sleepy after his long walk, said to the Monkey, "Let us make a wager for fun. You wager that you will sleep more soundly and longer and stay more still on your branch than I can. I will wager the same. The one to carry it through to be the winner."

The Monkey agreed to the proposal, and they settled themselves for the night. The Heron tucked his head under his wing and remained perfectly still, but the Monkey kept opening and shutting his eyes and peeping down at the Heron. After a short while he cried out: "It's so dark I am unable to see if you move or not."

The Heron made no reply. The Monkey couldn't be quiet. He fidgeted continually. He broke off bits of twig and threw them down on the

Heron; shook the branches, and did all he could to cause a disturbance. Still the Heron remained stock still.

"Are you moving?" shrieked the Monkey.

The Heron was really angry with the Monkey, whose restlessness made it impossible for him to sleep, and the Heron called up, "Be quiet and keep to your wager."

Now the Heron had a very harsh voice, which sounded still harsher when he raised it in anger, and the noise of it gave the Monkey such a start that he lost his hold of the branch and fell into the swamp. The Heron, hearing a great splash, thought some wild beast had scented them out and was swimming to the tree, and with a flap of his wings flew off in alarm.

The poor Monkey found himself alone and in a sorry plight. He made great efforts to get out of the swamp, but the more he struggled the deeper he sank till only his head showed above. He screamed and shouted for help, but in vain, and there he had to stay, not daring to move a pace now in case he become submerged in the soft mud altogether.

At daybreak a Wildcat slunk by and the Monkey called to the Wildcat and begged for help, saying, "If you will get me out of here, Brother, I will give you my flesh to eat."

"Very well," said the Wildcat, "I am hunting for my breakfast," and he came forward to the edge of the swamp and tried to fish the Monkey up. He fished and fished without being able to get hold of the Monkey, so he said, "I prefer to get my breakfast elsewhere," and stalked on.

"Do not abandon me," called the Monkey, and the Wildcat replied, "Another brother will be sure to pass, ask him to help you."

The Monkey waited anxiously for another brother, and sure enough after awhile he caught sight of a Jackal.

"Brother! Brother!" called the Monkey. "Halt! If you get me out of here you can eat my flesh."

And the Jackal made the same bargain with

the Monkey as had the Wildcat. However, he found the task more difficult than he supposed, and after making a good try he, too, told the Monkey he would rather get his meal elsewhere. And after a long time a Leopard tried but he, too, failed.

When a Tigress passed that afternoon, it was all the Monkey could do to attract her attention. But he managed to call in a husky voice, "Pray stop! Pray stop!" until she turned and saw him.

"What do you want of me?" she inquired.

"I want to get out of the swamp," wailed the Monkey. "If you will get me out I will give you my flesh to eat."

"I can get you out," said the Tigress. And she took her big paw and dragged him to her with ease. She then carried him to her den where her cubs were clamoring for dinner. The Tigress told the cubs to fetch sticks to make a fire, so that she could roast the Monkey.

"I nearly froze in the swamp," said the Monkey. "It will be a nice change to be roasted," and he pretended to be very pleased.

"I will have to get the mud off you before I put you on the spit," said the Tigress, and she took the Monkey outside and laid him out on a flat stone to dry in the sun. He was caked with sticky mud from his neck to the tip of his tail.

The Tigress then left the Monkey, who lay as if he were going to sleep, and she went to help the cubs gather the sticks. In the warm sun the Monkey soon recovered his voice, and when the Tigress moved away he began to sing. He sang these words:

"Blow, wind, blow, and bend the supple bamboo."

The Tigress heard him singing and came to ask what he was saying.

"I am singing a song," said the Monkey, "because I feel happy at being roasted by a hot fire after being so cold all night."

"Why do you ask the wind to blow if you are so cold?" said the Tigress.

"Those are just the words of the song," replied the Monkey. "It is very interesting when you think the wind can bend the tops of the bamboo."

The Tigress was satisfied with this explanation and returned to join the cubs, who wanted to know what the Monkey sang.

"The nonsense you would expect from such a silly creature, who could beg to be taken out of a swamp to be eaten," said the Tigress. "You don't want to learn anything from him," and she went into the den and busied herself laying the fire for kindling.

Suddenly the wind really began to blow, but the Tigress did not hear it, for she was using the bellows. So the wind blew and bent the bamboo over, and the Monkey instantly caught hold of the bamboo top, which sprang back, and he was carried swiftly out of danger.

When the Tigress came out with the cubs to bring him in to be roasted, there was not even one of his footprints to be seen.

"Wherever has the silly creature got to?" said the Tigress, looking about her in surprise at the Monkey's sudden disappearance. But however silly she may have called the Monkey, this did not prevent her or her cubs from going supperless that night to bed.

The Ghost Who Was Afraid of Being Bagged

❦❦❦

ONCE ON A TIME there lived a Barber who had
a wife. They did not live happily together, as the
wife always complained that she had not enough
to eat. Many were the scoldings which were in-
flicted upon the poor Barber.

The wife used often to say to her husband, "If
you had not the means to support a wife, why did
you marry me? People who have not means ought
not to indulge in the luxury of a wife. When I
was in my father's house I had plenty to eat, but
it seems that I have come to your house to fast.
Widows are the only ones who fast; I have become
a widow in your lifetime!"

She was not content with mere words; she got
very angry one day and struck her husband with
the broomstick. Stung with shame, and unhappy
with himself because of his wife's scolding and

beating, he left his house, with the implements of his craft, and vowed never to return and see his wife's face again till he had become rich.

He went from village to village, and towards nightfall came to the outskirts of a forest. He laid himself down at the foot of a tree, and spent many a sad hour in bemoaning his hard lot.

It so chanced that the tree, at the foot of which the Barber was lying, was dwelt in by a Ghost. The Ghost seeing a human being at the foot of the tree naturally thought of destroying him. With this intention the Ghost came out of the tree, and, with outspread arms and a gaping mouth, stood like a tall palmyra tree before the Barber, and said:

"Now, Barber, I am going to destroy you. Who will protect you?"

The Barber, though quaking in every limb through fear, and his hair standing erect, did not lose his presence of mind, but, with that promptitude and shrewdness which are characteristic of barbers, replied, "O spirit, no doubt you will destroy me! But—wait a bit and I'll show you how many ghosts *I* have captured this very night and put into my bag; and right glad am I to find you here, as I shall have one more ghost in my bag."

So saying, the Barber produced from his bag a small looking glass, which he always carried about with him along with his razors, his whet-stones, his strop, and other utensils, so that his customers could see whether their beards had been well shaved or not. He stood up, placed the looking glass right against the face of the Ghost, and said, "Here you see one Ghost which I have seized and bagged; I am going to put you also in the bag to keep this Ghost company."

The Ghost, seeing his own face in the looking glass, was convinced of the truth of what the Barber had said, and was filled with fear. He said to the Barber, "Oh, sir Barber, I'll do whatever you bid me, only do not put me into your bag. I'll give you whatever you want."

The Barber said, "You Ghosts are a faithless set, there is no trusting you. You will promise, and not give what you promise."

"Oh, sir," replied the Ghost, "be merciful to me; I'll bring to you whatever you order; and if I do not bring it, then put me into your bag."

"Very well," said the Barber, "bring me just now one thousand gold mohurs; and by tomorrow night you must raise a granary behind my house, and fill it with paddy. Go and get the gold mohurs immediately; and if you fail to do my bidding you will certainly be put into my bag."

The Ghost gladly consented to the conditions. He went away, and in the course of a short time returned with a bag containing a thousand gold mohurs.

The Barber was delighted beyond measure at the sight of the gold mohurs. He then told the Ghost to see to it that by the following night a granary was erected behind his house and filled with paddy.

It was during the small hours of the morning that the Barber, loaded with the heavy treasure, knocked at the door of his house. His wife, who was sorry for having in a fit of rage struck her husband with the broomstick, got out of bed and unbolted the door. Her surprise was great when she saw her husband pour out of the bag a glittering heap of gold mohurs.

The next night the poor Ghost, through fear of being bagged, raised a large granary behind the Barber's house and spent the livelong night in carrying on his back large bundles of paddy till the granary was filled up to the brim.

The Uncle of this terrified Ghost, seeing his worthy nephew carrying on his back the large bundles of paddy, asked what the matter was. The Ghost related what had happened.

The Uncle-Ghost then said, "You fool, you think the Barber can bag you! The Barber is a cunning fellow; he has cheated you, like the simpleton you are."

"You doubt," said the Nephew-Ghost, "the power of the Barber! Come and see."

The Uncle-Ghost then went to the Barber's house, and peeped into it through a window. The Barber, knowing from the blast of wind which the arrival of the Ghost had produced that a Ghost was at the window, placed full before it the self-same looking glass, saying, "Come now, I'll put you also into the bag!"

The Uncle-Ghost, seeing his own face in the looking glass, got quite frightened, and promised that very night to raise another granary and to fill it, not this time with paddy, but with rice.

So in two nights the Barber became a rich man, and lived happily with his wife, begetting sons and daughters.

The Wolf
and the Blacksmith

❀❀❀

LONG AGO in Poland, when animals could talk, there lived in a tiny hut in the middle of a dense and silent forest a very holy man, Saint Stanislaw. He was so gentle that the wild beasts of the forest —the Lion, the Bear, and even the Rabbit—often stopped to talk with him. Always the Saint listened to them with sympathy; always he gave them good advice.

One day as the Saint walked in the woods, a large gray Wolf approached him and said to him:

"Great Saint, I have a favor to ask of you. Many kinds of meat have I tasted in my lifetime. When I was young, before I was strong enough to bring down a stag, I had lamb, goat, and sheep. I have had venison to eat and even the meat of the horse."

"There is no doubt that you have fared better than your cousin the Jackal," replied Saint Stanislaw.

"No, that I have not! I have not tasted human flesh, and the Jackal says it is very sweet."

"Human flesh is bitter and tough. Do not think of tasting it!"

"Saint Stanislaw, surely you are mistaken. Would my cousin the Jackal say it is sweet if it were not?"

"The Jackal is cunning and wishes to turn your attention from hunting the tender lambs and the savory deer."

But the Wolf insisted. "Please let me taste it just this once."

"You are going to be sorry," Saint Stanislaw warned him.

"I do not care. Only let me satisfy my curiosity."

At last the Saint consented. "I shall then permit you to devour a human being—"

"Thank you, great Saint, thank you!"

"But, Wolf, there is this condition: You may not eat a little boy with a book under his arm going to school. You may not eat an old man whose beard and hair are white like mine. If you must devour a human being, it will have to be a blacksmith. Is it a bargain?"

"It is a bargain."

Greedily, the Wolf licked his lips and sped away through the woods like an arrow. At the edge of the road he sat down to wait for the Blacksmith the Saint had permitted him to eat.

He listened, looked—and saw that someone was coming down the road. Eagerly he called out:

"Who are you?"

"Can't you see that I am a little boy with a book under my arm on the way to school?"

"Hurry, then," said the Wolf. "A schoolboy is good for nothing."

The Wolf waited as patiently as an empty stomach permitted.

He listened, looked—and saw that someone was coming down the road. He stretched out his muzzle and called:

"Ho, there! Who are you, now, good fellow?"

"I am a very old man, so old that even with the help of this staff I can hardly drag one foot after the other. I am going to the next village on the other side of the woods to pray in the church. I may never get there. A child and an old man find even a short distance very long."

"God be with you and take you to the little church, Grandfather. I am watching for someone else."

Once more the Wolf sat down to wait for the Blacksmith.

He listened, looked—and saw that someone was coming down the road.

At last! At last!

A bold young Blacksmith wearing a leather jerkin strode along in a happy carefree manner. The Wolf began to sharpen his teeth for him and called out:

"Oho! Who are you, now?"

"Don't you see that I am a big, strong blacksmith, a jolly good fellow who works with a will? But what are you sitting here for?"

"Blacksmith, I am waiting to eat you up!"

"What for?"

"Because I am hungry, and Saint Stanislaw has said that I may devour a Blacksmith."

"Friend Wolf, in the village yonder I shall get you the sweetest lamb in the market."

"Ah, no, Blacksmith, I do not trust your promises. Besides, I know how lamb tastes."

"Then, Wolf, before I die, let me wash myself in the pool beyond the bushes. My face is black with soot, and my hairy arms and thick hair are powdered with ashes."

"Very well, Blacksmith. Wash yourself, but be quick. And remember, if you try to escape, I will tear you in pieces."

The Blacksmith plunged through the bushes to the pool, but instead of washing himself at once, he quickly cut a stout stick and buttoned it under his jacket. Busily and noisily then he splashed his large hands in the pool and raised them dripping, again and again, to his grimy face until he had washed it thoroughly.

Then he hastened back to the Wolf and said: "Friend Wolf, I am ready at last, but I am dripping wet. Perhaps you will permit me to dry my face and hands on your long furry tail."

"I am not at all comfortable when my fur is wet. However, since I am about to devour you, I shall allow you this once to dry yourself on the hairs of my tail."

Saying this, the Wolf turned around.

At once the Blacksmith seized the heavy tail

and wrapped it tightly three times around his wrists. Then he pulled out the heavy club and beat the Wolf without mercy, until the poor beast lay half dead in the road, covered with bruises and welts.

The Blacksmith the Wolf had intended to eat went whistling on his way, with his hands in his pockets.

Several hours later the Wolf came to his senses and managed to drag himself back to the woods. He howled mournfully again and again: "Ow! Ow!"—for at every step his body ached the more.

Saint Stanislaw in his bare hut heard the wailing of the injured Wolf and set forth to find him and help him.

"Ow! Ow! Great Saint, human flesh is very bitter," cried the Wolf. "Oh, I am sick. Human flesh is like gall."

"Is it really so bad as that?"

"Great Saint, you do not know, you have never tasted it. Lamb and venison are good, but the flesh of a Blacksmith—! Oh, never mention it to me again!"

The Story of Yukpachen

❦❦❦

YUKPACHEN WAS a foolish fellow. He meant well, but he was foolish, utterly and absurdly foolish. All his intentions were good, but his actions showed that what he did was done without thought. Fortunately for Yukpachen, luck favored him. Now I will tell you what happened to Yukpachen one day of his foolish life.

Yukpachen was walking along with never so much as a care in his empty head when he saw a pony galloping towards him.

"Hi," called the owner of the pony, "my pony has bolted. Stop him, stop him."

"I will stop him," said Yukpachen, and he picked up a sharp stone and threw it with all his might at the pony's leg. Certainly he stopped the pony running, for he broke its leg.

"There, I have stopped him running," he cried cheerfully. "He won't run off again in a hurry."

This was quite true, of course, but the owner of the pony was very cross, and well he may have been. He got hold of Yukpachen by the arm and said:

"I will take you to the King and tell him what you have done."

"Come along," said Yukpachen happily. "It is a fine day for an outing, and I would like to see the King."

So away they went. When they had walked some distance they came to a stream. In the middle of the stream was a man laden with bundles. He was so heavily laden that he was obliged to carry his ax in his mouth.

"Oh, Brother," called Yukpachen, "how deep is the water?"

The man naturally could not answer, so Yukpachen shouted again.

"Brother, tell us how deep is the water."

At this the man became irritated and opened his mouth to say something, and the ax fell from his mouth into the stream.

"I have lost my good ax," said the man angrily. "You shall come with me to the King. I will tell him how it happened."

"Willingly, Brother," said Yukpachen. "We are now on our way to the King. Let us get there with all possible speed."

They had not gone far when they came to a wall.

"A wall," said Yukpachen. "There is only one way to get over it quickly," and he took a flying leap.

On the other side of the wall a man was sitting weaving. Yukpachen landed on his head and killed him instantly. The man's wife, who happened to be working in the fields near by, saw Yukpachen jump on her husband's head.

"You have killed my husband," she screamed. "You shall be brought before the King."

"How sad," said Yukpachen. "I am sure the King will be sorry to hear it. But console yourself, he died at least easily."

So the owner of the runaway pony, the owner of the ax, and the dead man's wife took Yukpachen to the King.

"O King," said the owner of the pony, "I bring before you a man who, when I shouted to him to stop my pony bolting, took up a sharp stone and threw it at the animal's leg, injuring him in such a manner as to make him useless to me. Pray judge him according to his wickedness."

"O King," said the owner of the ax, "I bring before you this man who saw me fording a stream so burdened with bundles that I was forced to carry my ax between my teeth. Yet he questioned me—not once but twice—as to the depth of the water. I opened my mouth to tell him to close his, and my ax slipped from the grip of my teeth into the water and is lost to me. Pray judge him as you see fit."

"O King," said the woman on whose husband's head Yukpachen had jumped, "I bring before you a man who leaped over a high wall onto my husband's head, thus killing him and leaving me husbandless. Pray give him the punishment he so richly deserves."

"In the first case," said the King, addressing Yukpachen, "I order the owner of the pony to have his tongue cut off for shouting to you on the road to catch his pony for him. And you, Yukpachen, you shall have your hands cut off at the wrists for throwing the stone and injuring the pony's leg."

"O King," pleaded the owner of the pony, "I beseech you to let this man off, as his action was foolish, not wicked."

"In the second case," said the King, "I order that all the teeth of the man carrying the ax shall be drawn for allowing the ax to slip into the water, and that your tongue, Yukpachen, shall be pulled out from the roots for asking needless questions."

"O King," said the owner of the ax, "grant this man pardon. True, he shouted to me, but not with any intent to cause me loss. I therefore, plead with you to let him go unpunished."

"In the third case," said the King, "this poor woman wishes you to be punished as you deserve. I order Yukpachen, that your legs shall be chopped off for jumping the wall, and that you shall marry your victim's wife so that she shall not remain husbandless."

"O King," said the woman, "his punishment is far greater than he deserves. Grant him pardon."

The King thereupon ordered them to return to their homes and trouble him no further with their grievances. So Yukpachen went unpunished, Yukpachen the lucky, Yukpachen the foolish, Yukpachen the well-meaning fellow.

Yehl Outwits Kanukh*

❧❧❧

KANUKH WAS the greatest of all sorcerers and the oldest. He guarded the one deep, pure spring. There was no fresh water in the world except in this one spring.

Now the Thlinkits had drunk salt water for so long that their tears and blood to this day taste of salt. They longed for only a taste of the sweet water, and prayed to Yehl to get water from Kanukh, so that they, too, might have springs. Therefore Yehl put on his magic bird skin and flew to the island far toward the east where Kanukh guarded the well of sweet water.

But Kanukh by his arts knew of the coming of Yehl and raised a tempest of such great blackness and fury that Yehl was glad to descend to the earth. He took off his magic bird skin and the storm ceased. The sun shone. Yehl made himself a canoe, and the canoe of itself bore him toward the island.

*Retold from *How Yehl Outwitted Kanukh and Gave Fresh Water to the Thlinkits.*

Kanukh paddled out to meet him saying, "Who art thou?"

"I am the raven, bold and cunning," answered Yehl. "Who art thou?"

"I am the wolf, cunning and bold," said Kanukh. "What canst thou do?" asked he of Yehl.

"All things I can do," answered Yehl very proudly.

"Then save thyself," said Kanukh; and he put on his tall hat of sorcery, and immediately there arose an impenetrable fog, white as wool and so cold it chilled the marrow. Yehl was frightened. Earth and sky and sea were blotted out, and he seemed adrift in nothingness; great icebergs loomed suddenly above him; from them came the calls and cries of the devil spirits; he could see their eyes. Out of the air arose shrieks. Ghosts swept across him and through him. His blood froze. He cried aloud, "Oh, Kanukh! Thou art greater than I." Then the sun drove away the fog and the sea was calm.

Kanukh took him into his canoe and they sped to the shore. Kanukh had a great feast spread and they feasted for three days, drinking deeply of the delicious sweet water. Yehl thought how he might steal some water; but Kanukh watched him always. And he knew what was in Yehl's mind.

Now there had been given to Yehl, for his help-

mate and companion, a maiden, plump and
smooth as a young seal and very beautiful. She
told Yehl that he must amuse Kanukh until the
time of the new moon when the moon became
a thread in the sky, and on that night and that
night alone, Kanukh would be overpowered with
sleep.

Therefore Yehl amused Kanukh. He shot the
arrow and threw the spear—never missing the
smallest mark. He fought and slew the giant
Devilfish, which could reach with its arms to the
top of the highest cliffs. He told many tales of his
adventures.

Kanukh wished to be rid of Yehl for the time
of his sleeping was drawing near. One day at a

feast he challenged Yehl to slay the Bear Demon, which dwelt in the mountains. Kanukh knew that Yehl would be killed by the Demon or that the fight would keep Yehl away at the time of the new moon.

Yehl looked into the heart of Kanukh and laughed, saying, "I will bring you his hide, upon which you may rest yourself when you sleep."

With the magic mantle upon his shoulders and his magic bow in his hand, Yehl set forth upon his quest. Kanukh, by his sorcery, sent a great tempest upon the path of Yehl. The trees groaned and hurled their branches upon the ground, snow and ice stripped the trees, and the air was black. But Yehl, flying with his magic mantle, mounted into the regions of the sun and sat upon a cloud, and waited for the earth to appear. At last the tempest stopped, and far in the mountains, he came upon a bear's footprint, fifteen feet in length and five feet in width.

Yehl followed these tracks for they were easy to follow—the trees were broken like twigs where they passed. Yehl looked ahead and he saw a mountain bare of snow. As he looked, the brown mountain moved; and the heart of Yehl choked him. This was the great Bear Demon.

When the Bear Demon saw Yehl he bellowed so that the earth shook; then he hurled himself

upon Yehl, who shot arrow upon arrow so fast
that they went from the bow to the heart of the
Bear in a single stream; but the Bear would not
die. Yehl turned and fled. Below him was a great
cliff; he fitted his magic mantle close and launched
himself down into the air. Down also fell the
Bear, striking the rocks and sweeping away the
forest and the earth for many miles. The great
Bear Demon lay dead.

Yehl took the skin, the head, and the claws,
and flew to Kanukh; and before Kanukh he spread
the great field of fur.

It so happened that it was the evening of the
new moon. Kanukh was angry. He spread another
feast for Yehl, and set apart another house for
him, and sent other maidens to attend him; then,
feeling the sleep come over him, he had his couch
made upon the cover of the well and there fell
asleep.

Yehl at his feast called continually for the sweet
water, but presently there was none to give him.
"I will see to that," said he; and, going to the well,
he smeared Kanukh with filth and returned to his
feast.

When all were asleep, just before the stars went
out of the sky in the morning, there was a cry of
anger from Kanukh. Yehl hastened there, unseen,
and saw Kanukh hurrying to the sea to wash him-

self; for it was abhorrent that filth should be near to the sacred well.

While he was absent, Yehl dipped from the well a bowl of the clear water and on his magic wings flew away; but Kanukh, as a huge bird, pursued and attacked him so that when Yehl was over the land of the Thlinkits he was forced to drop the bowl of water, and it fell. The great drops made lakes and the small drops made springs throughout all the land.

So it was that fresh water came to the Thlinkits. The maiden who was Yehl's friend in the house of Kanukh became a gull, and flies over the water seeking him and crying; but Yehl went away into the Eternal Land, whence he will return some day to the Thlinkits.

May we all live as Yehl lived.

How the Devil Was Outsmarted by the Man

❦❦❦

ONCE UPON A TIME there was a poor Man who had a hard time making a living. All he possessed were his little hut at the edge of the village, old and weatherbeaten, and a tiny field on the side of a hill. Five hungry children cried for food and the poor Mother had nothing to give them. Most of the time, all they had to eat was bread and water, the bread so hard and dry that it crunched between their teeth.

One day the Mother, who had received some flour for work she had done, wanted to bake bread, and, as there was nothing with which to make a fire, the Father said he would go into the woods and gather some dry sticks. So he went to the forest and was searching for dry branches, when who should stand before him but the Devil!

Now the Man knew who stood before him and had the good sense to keep his wits.

"What are you searching all the trees for?" asked the Devil.

"For a young linden, my friend," answered the Man. "From its fiber I shall make a rope with a noose on the end with which to catch Devils. Such a rope will be a fine thing, for they cannot escape from that."

At this the Devil, because he was foolish, became much frightened.

"Oh, don't do that! Truly that would be bad for us. What can I give you to leave us in peace?"

"Bring me a bag of gold!" answered the Man.

The Devil disappeared, but in a few minutes returned with the bag of gold, gave it to the Man, and hurried off to hell rejoicing.

There he said to the other Devils, "My dear Brothers, I have saved you from a terrible danger."

But, when he told them all, they only laughed at him.

"How foolish you are to give a bag of gold for nothing! Now you shall go back to that man and wrestle with him for it!"

So the Devil came up to earth, sought out the poor Man, and said that he had given him too

much for his favor; that they should wrestle together, the stronger one to have the gold.

The Man, cunning as a fox, agreed at once.

"I have a grandfather," he said, "an old man
ninety and nine years old. If you overcome him, it
will be the same as though you overcame me."

And he led the Devil into the woods, among the
rocks, where a bear had his den.

"There lies my grandfather; do you see him?"

The Devil went bravely up to the bear,
wakened him, and said, "Come, Grandfather, let
us wrestle."

But the bear quickly snatched the Devil with
his great paws and hugged him till his bones began to crack. The Devil had all he could do to
get away, and straight as an arrow, he flew back
to hell.

"I want nothing to do with that old man. He
has a grandfather, an old man ninety and nine
years old, who has so much strength that it is
terrible. What must the grandson's be?"

But the Devils were not satisfied, and all insisted that he must return to the earth and again
contend with the Man.

So the Devil again sought out the Man and
asked him to race, the money to go to the swifter.

The Man, a thorough rogue, consented at once.

"I have a little son, a tiny fellow, who is not yet a year old. If you outrun him, it will be the same as though you had outrun me."

And he led the Devil to the edge of the woods where a rabbit lived among the bushes.

"There lies my little son; do you see him?"

The Devil went to waken the rabbit.

"Get up, little fellow, let us race."

But the rabbit did not wait for the devil to get ready. He sprang from his hiding place and ran. The Devil started after him and ran as hard as he could, but was not able to catch up. Directly in their path was a gorge, deep and rocky, with a stream at the bottom.

The rabbit leaped; the Devil leaped after him,

only to fall splashing into the water. Crawling out all bruised and dripping, he looked about for the rabbit, which was just then scampering over the other side. So the Devil went limping back to hell.

"I want nothing more to do with that man. He has a son, a little fellow not yet a year old, who runs like the wind. How must the father run?"

But because the Devils all insisted, this foolish one had to return to the earth a third time to contend with the man. This time to whistle.

The Man was willing at once.

"Whistle!" ordered the Devil.

"No," said the Man. "You should whistle first. Just you begin and do your best."

The Devil whistled once; leaves fell from the trees. He whistled the second time, more loudly; twigs dropped off. He whistled the third time, and great branches broke.

"Oh, your whistling is weak," said the Man. "When I whistle, the trees will fall, the noise will deafen you!"

At that the Devil begged the Man to tie up his ears. The Man gladly tied a kerchief not only over his ears, but over his eyes, too. Then, picking up one of the strongest of the broken branches, he whistled and struck the Devil over the head with it.

"See, I told you the trees would fall!"

He whistled the second time and brought the branch down onto the Devil's head still harder. At this the Devil begged the man not to whistle again.

"No, I must whistle again. As you whistled three times, I will, too," said the Man.

He whistled the third time and struck with all his might. At this the Devil tore the bandage from his eyes and, without even looking for the uprooted trees, ran straight off to hell.

The bag of gold was left with the Man and he never saw that Devil again.

Teeth and No-Teeth

❧❧❧

SHAH ALI DESIRED TO SEE the hungriest man in
his kingdom, and find out how much food such
a man could eat at a meal. So he let it be known
that on a certain day he would dine with his Courtiers in the open air, in front of the palace. At
the appointed hour, tables were laid and dinner
was served, in the presence of a vast crowd.

After the first course, the Shah mounted a dais,
and said: "My loyal subjects! You see what a
splendid dinner I have. I should like to share it
with those among you who are really hungry, and
have not eaten for a long time, so tell me truly
which is the hungriest of you all, and bid him
come forward."

Two men appeared from the crowd: an old
man of fifty and a young man of twenty-seven.
The former was gray-haired and feeble, the latter
was fresh and of athletic build.

"How is it that you are hungry?" asked the
Shah of the Old Man.

"I am old, toil has worn me out, my children are dead, and I have eaten nothing for three days."

"And you?" said the Shah, turning to the Young Man.

"I could not find work, and as I am a hearty young man I am ashamed to beg, so I, too, have not eaten for three days."

The Shah ordered them to be given food. The hungry men ate as fast as they could, watching each other intently. Suddenly the Old Man and the Young Man both stopped eating and began to weep.

"Why do you weep?" asked the Shah in astonishment.

"I have no teeth," said the Old Man, "and while I am mumbling my food this young man eats up everything."

"And why are you weeping?" the Shah asked the Young Man.

"He is telling lies, Your Majesty; while I am chewing my meat the old man gulps down everything whole."

How the Hodja
Outwits the Shah Ali

❦❦❦

ONCE UPON A TIME, there reigned in one of the
realms of the East a Shah named Ali, a man of
amiable and merry character. The Shah loved to
set his folk riddles to guess; prizes were given to
those who guessed the answers. Once the servants
of the Shah made known to the people, that Ali
had promised three hundred pieces of gold to him
who should tell His Majesty such a story that he
would be forced to reply: THAT IS IMPOSSI-
BLE.

This announcement created great excitement,
and men, women, and children all alike set themselves to think out such a story. The day of the
competition dawned at last, and the vast square
before the palace was crowded with a curious
throng. At the appointed hour, Shah Ali appeared,
surrounded by his guard, and music from the
band filled the air.

After greeting his people, the Shah sat down on a throne, opposite the platform on which the candidates were to stand while they told the Shah their stories. Heralds gave out the challenge, and a wit of the town mounted the platform and loudly said: "Shah! A courier has just galloped into the town and told me a most astonishing piece of news, to wit, that at dawn this morning, twenty versts from your capital, the moon fell from the sky to the ground, and burned two and twenty villages to ashes." The Shah thought a moment, and then replied: "That is possible."

His place was taken by the Shah's physician, who shouted:

"Most illustrious Shah! In your harem a most astounding event has just happened—your first wife, your beloved Zuleika, has just given birth to a suckling pig covered with bristles." The Shah considered, and then replied: "That is possible." The doctor fled in shame, and the people laughed more loudly than before.

After the doctor came an astrologer, who said: "Most noble Shah! In observing the courses of the stars I have discovered a woeful piece of news; an awful fate awaits you. O King, you will soon have horns like a goat, and claws like a panther, you will lose the power of speech, and flee from us into the woods, where you will dwell exactly

seven years and three months." To him likewise
the Shah replied: "That is possible," and he, too,
disappeared, amid the jeers of the mob.

The competition lasted throughout the whole
of that day and the next, to the delight of the
people, until at last they thought of getting a certain Hodja, Nasr-Eddin, a wit well known
throughout the East, to oppose the Shah.

On the third, and last, day appeared the Hodja,
tattered and almost naked, dragging with him
two great clay jars. Addressing the Shah, he
said: "Hail to the commander of the faithful,
blessed be thy name! Thou shalt reign yet a hundred years, and the love and confidence of thy
subjects will increase yearly."

"That is possible," said the Shah.

"That the confidence your subjects repose in
you is unbounded is evident from a fact which I
am about to relate—you will doubtless deign to
listen,"

"That is possible," said the Shah.

"Your late father (God rest his soul!) was
very friendly with my late father (may the
Prophet give him a place in Paradise!)"

"That is possible," said the Shah.

"Listen to me, O Shah! When your father went
forth to war with the unbeliever, he was so poor
that he could not raise an army."

"That is possible," said the Shah.

"Not only is it possible but true, for, owing to his want of money, he borrowed from my father these two jars full of gold pieces, and promised on his royal word that you, O Shah, would pay your father's debt to me."

Shah Ali burst into laughter, and said: "THAT IS IMPOSSIBLE! Your father was a tatterdemalion like yourself, and never saw two jars of gold *even* in his dreams. Take your three hundred pieces of gold, and the devil take you. You rascal, you have outwitted me."

Heavy Collar and the Ghost Woman

❦❦❦

IT IS TOLD among the Bloods that once when Heavy Collar was on his homeward way from a scouting trip, he saw at a distance three buffalo close to a cut bank. Heavy Collar went out to kill one of these bulls, and when he had come close to them, he shot one and killed it right there. He cut it up, and, as he was hungry, he went down into a ravine below him, to roast a piece of meat; for he had left his party a long way behind, and night was now coming on.

As he was roasting the meat, he thought, "I am tired and it is a pity I did not bring one of my young men with me. He could go up on that hill and get some hair from that bull's head, and I could wipe out my gun." While he sat there thinking this and talking to himself, a bunch of this buffalo hair came over him through the air, and fell on the ground right in front of him.

When this happened, it frightened him a little; for there were many war parties about. He thought that some of his enemies were close by, and had thrown the bunch of hair at him. After a little while when no enemy came, he took the hair, and cleaned his gun and loaded it, and then he sat and watched for a time. He was uneasy, and at length decided that he would go on further up the river, to see what he could discover. He went on, up the stream, until he came to the mouth of the river. It was now very late in the night, and he was very tired, so he crept into a large bunch of ryegrass to hide and sleep for the night.

The summer before this, the Blackfeet had been camped in this bottom, and a woman had been killed in this very same patch of ryegrass where Heavy Collar had lain down to rest. He did not know this, but still he was troubled that night. He could not sleep. He could always hear something, but what it was he could not make out. He tried to go to sleep, but as soon as he dozed off he kept thinking he heard something. He spent the night there, and in the morning when it became light, there he saw right beside him in the ryegrass the skeleton of the woman who had been killed the summer before.

He went on. All day long as he was traveling, he kept thinking about his having slept by the woman's bones. It troubled him. He could not forget it. At the same time he was very tired, because he had walked so far and had slept so little.

When night came, he crossed over to an island in the river to camp for the night. At one end of the island he found a large tree that had drifted down and lodged itself in the sand, and in a fork of this tree he built his fire. He sat with his back to the fire, warming himself, but all the time he was thinking about the bones he had slept beside the night before.

As he sat there, all at once he heard over beyond the tree, on the other side of the fire, a sound as if

something were being dragged toward him along the ground. It sounded as if a piece of lodge were being dragged over the grass. It came closer and closer. Closer and closer.

Heavy Collar was scared. He was afraid to turn his head and look back to see what it was that was coming. He heard the noise come up to the tree in which his fire was built, and then it stopped, and all at once he heard someone whistling a tune. He turned around and looked toward the sound. And there, sitting on the other fork of the tree, exactly opposite him, was the pile of bones by which he had slept, only now all together in the shape of a skeleton.

Now the skeleton was a Ghost. The Ghost sat on the old dead limb and whistled its tune, and as it whistled, it swung its legs in time to the tune.

When Heavy Collar saw this, his heart almost melted away. At length he mustered up courage, and said: "O Ghost, go away, and do not trouble me. I am very tired; I want to rest."

The Ghost paid no attention to him, but kept on whistling, swinging its legs in time to the tune.

Four times he prayed to her, saying: "O Ghost, take pity on me! Go away and leave me alone. I am tired; I want to rest."

The more he prayed, the more the Ghost whistled and seemed pleased, swinging her legs, and turning her head from side to side, sometimes looking down at him, and sometimes up at the stars, and all the time whistling.

When he saw that she took no notice of what he said, Heavy Collar got angry and said: "Well, Ghost, you do not listen to my prayers, and I shall have to shoot you to drive you away." And with that he seized his gun, threw it to his shoulders, sighted along the barrel, and shot right at the Ghost.

When he shot at her, she fell over backward into the darkness, screaming out: "O Heavy Collar, you have shot me, you have killed me! You dog, Heavy Collar! There is no place on this earth where you can go that I will not find you; no place where you can hide that I will not come."

As she fell back and said this, Heavy Collar sprang to his feet, and ran away as fast as he could.

She called after him: "I have been killed once, and now you have tried to kill me again. O Heavy Collar!"

As he ran away, he could still hear her angry words following him, until at last they died away in the distance. He ran all night long, and whenever he stopped to breathe and listen, he seemed to hear in the distance the echoes of her voice. All he could hear was, "O Heavy Collar!"

And then he would rush away again. He ran until he was all tired out, and by this time it was daylight. He was now quite a long way from home. He was very sleepy, but dared not lie down, for he remembered that the Ghost had said that she would follow him. He kept walking on for some time, and then sat down to rest, and at once fell asleep.

When he awoke from his sleep, he started straight for the Blood Camp to meet the rest of his party.

When his party reached the camp, one of them went up on top of a hill to watch. After a time, as he looked down the river, he saw two persons coming, and as they came nearer, he saw that one of them was Heavy Collar, and by his side was a woman.

The watcher called up the rest of the party, and said to them: "Here comes our chief. He has had luck. He is bringing a woman with him. If he brings her into camp, we will take her away from him."

When the two persons had come close, they could see Heavy Collar was walking fast, and the woman would walk by his side a little way, trying to keep up, and then would fall behind, and then trot along to catch up to him again. Just before the pair reached camp there was a deep ravine that they had to cross. They went down into this side by side, and then Heavy Collar came up out of it alone, and came on into camp.

When he got there, all the young men began to laugh at him and to call out, "Heavy Collar, where is the woman?"

Heavy Collar looked at them for a moment, and then said: "Why, I have no woman with me. I do not understand what you are talking about."

One of the men said: "Why, that woman that you had with you just now. We all saw her, and it is no use to deny that she was with you. Come now, where is she?"

When they said this, Heavy Collar's heart grew very heavy, for he knew that it must have been the Ghost Woman; and he told them the story. Some of the young men did not believe this, and they ran down to the ravine, where they had last seen the woman. There they saw in the soft dirt the tracks made by Heavy Collar, when he went down into the ravine, but there were no other tracks near his, where they had seen the woman walking.

When they found that it was a Ghost that had come along with Heavy Collar, they decided to go back to their main camp without any delay. They set out immediately and at last they found the camp.

That night, after they had reached camp, they were inviting each other to feasts. It was getting late and the moon was shining brightly, when one of the Bloods called out for Heavy Collar to come and eat with him.

Heavy Collar shouted, "Yes, I will be there pretty soon."

He got up and went out of the lodge, and went a little way from it, and sat down. While he was sitting there, a big bear walked out of the brush close to him. Heavy Collar felt around him for a stone to throw at the bear, so as to scare it away, for he thought it had not seen him. As he was feeling about, his hand came upon a piece of bone, and he threw this over at the bear, and hit it.

Then the bear spoke, and said: "Well, well, well, Heavy Collar; you have killed me once, and now here you are hitting me. Where is there a place in this world where you can hide from me? I will find you, I don't care where you may go."

When Heavy Collar heard this, he knew it was the Ghost Woman, and he jumped up and ran toward his lodge, calling out, "Run! Run! A ghost bear is upon us!"

All the people in the camp ran to his lodge, so that it was crowded full of people. There was a big fire in the lodge, and the wind was blowing hard from the west. Men, women, and children were huddled together in the lodge, and were very much afraid of the Ghost.

They could hear her walking toward the lodge, grumbling, and saying: "I will kill all these dogs. Not one of them shall get away." The sounds kept coming closer and closer, until they were right at the lodge door. Then she said, "I will smoke you to death."

And as she said this, she moved the poles, so that the wings of the lodge turned where the wind could blow in freely through the smoke hole. All this time she was threatening terrible things against them.

The lodge began to get full of smoke, and the children were crying, and the smoke was suffocating them. So they said: "Let us lift one man up here inside, and let him try to turn the poles, so that the lodge will get clear of smoke." They raised a man up, and he was standing on the shoulders of the others when the Ghost suddenly hit the lodge a blow and said, "Unh!" This scared the people who were holding the man, and they jumped and let him go, and he fell down. Then the people said: "It is no use; she is determined to smoke us to death." And all the time the smoke was getting thicker and thicker in the lodge.

Heavy Collar said: "Is it possible that she can destroy us? Is there no one here who has some

strong dream power that can overcome this
Ghost?"

His mother said: "I will try to do something.
I am older than any of you, and I will see what I
can do." So she got down her medicine bundle
and painted herself, and got out a pipe and filled
it and lighted it, and stuck the stem out through
the lodge door, and sat there and began to pray
to the Ghost Woman.

She said: "O Ghost, take pity on us, and go
away. We have never wronged you, but you are
troubling us and frightening our children. Accept
what I offer you, and leave us alone."

A voice came from behind the lodge and said:
"No, No, No, you dogs, I will not listen to you.
Everyone of you must die."

The old woman repeated her prayer: "O
Ghost, take pity on us. Accept this smoke and
go away."

Then the Ghost said: "How can you expect me
to smoke, when I am way back here? Bring that
pipe out here. I have no long bill like a bird to
reach round the lodge."

So the old woman went out of the lodge door,
and reached out the stem of the pipe as far as she
could reach around toward the back of the lodge.

The Ghost said: "No, I do not wish to go
around there to where you have that pipe. If you

want me to smoke it, you must bring it here."

The old woman went around the lodge toward her, and the Ghost Woman began to back away, and said, "No, I do not smoke that kind of pipe." And when the Ghost started away, the old woman followed her, and she could not help herself.

She called out, "O my children, the Ghost is carrying me off!"

Heavy Collar rushed out, and called to the others, "Come, and help me take my mother from the Ghost."

He grasped his mother about the waist and held her, and another man took him by the waist, and another him, until they were all strung out, one behind the other, and all following the old woman, who was following the Ghost Woman, who was walking away.

All at once the old woman let go of the pipe, and fell over dead. The Ghost disappeared, and they were troubled no more by the Ghost Woman.

The Bee

❦❦❦

ONE DAY King Solomon lay down beneath a fig tree in his garden to sleep his afternoon sleep, and two body-servants stood silently by his pillow, waving their fans to ward off the flies. The King's eyelids had scarcely closed when a small roving bee passed by. It gave no heed to the fans but alighted and sat on the King's nose and stung it. Solomon awoke and leapt up. He knew what had been done to him. His anger was kindled, for the pain in his nose was as sharp as the point of a knife; moreover his nose swelled and turned as red as a pomegranate. Solomon hunted for that rebellious daughter to punish her as her insolence deserved, and he sought and he groped, but she was nowhere to be found, for the wanton creature had fled for her life and hidden herself.

Every minute the King's nose grew more swollen and bloated. It soon grew as big as a cucumber. The King's heart raged within him and his countenance turned to vinegar.

Then in his fury he commanded that every bee should at once be brought before him, together with every hornet, and every wasp, and every fly, and every gnat, and every midge, even to the very tiniest creature in his garden and the regions about both near and far.

Then came trembling out of the nests and hives every bee and every hornet and every gnat and every buzzing creature after its kind; and they came in clouds from far and near, alighting before the King by swarms and swarms and by companies and companies, like the stars of heaven for multitude, each queen bee with her swarm and each company with its leader. All were in a panic, all in confusion, all of them buzzing, and

all of them amazed and rushing about to find out what was the matter:

"What is this-s-s-s? And why is this-s-s-s?"

And the King, goaded by the heat of his fury and his inflamed nose, stamped his feet and cried out, "Silence!"

An awed silence fell upon all: none stirred a wing or buzzed. Then they perceived, every one of them, and knew that of a truth the King's anger was great and terrible, exceedingly great and terrible.

The King's nose had gone on growing and swelling until it had become like a waterskin, filled to its very spout with sharp points of glass and thin, white-hot needles, striving to pierce their way out. In his pain and burning anger the King cried out,

"What son of Belial or what perverse and rebellious daughter among you hath thought fit to do to the King such a thing as this?"

And as he said "this" he touched his waterskin of a nose with his thumb, as if he would say, "See what indignity ye have done to the King!"

For a moment the bees held their peace; they were greatly alarmed in their fear of the King, and by his rebuke. But they soon recovered courage and a soft murmur spread from company to company, a murmur of surprise and perplexity:

"Ah! Ah! Who ever could it be that would do

this abominable thing? Who did this-s-s-s? Who
did this-s-s-s?"

While they were quietly buzzing, one little Bee
flew up out of the throng. It flew in a straight line
until it reached the King. Then it stopped and
said,

"Here am I, my lord the King: I am the cul-
prit!"

"Thou?" roared Solomon like a lion, while his
nose flamed like a torch. "And on the nose of the
King! Didst thou neither reverence my nose nor
dread my anger?"

"Oh, my lord the King, let there be no anger!
Be it far from the daughter of thy handmaid ever
to alight presumptuously on the nose of the Lord's
Anointed, except it had been in foolishness or
error! I am but a young and tender bee: my days
are few in number; and foolish, most foolish, am
I. Not yet have I learned to tell the difference
between a flower and a nose, or between one nose
and another—particularly the nose of my lord the
King, that nose with its lilylike fragrance and its
applelike grace. Should it be accounted a crime
in a bee, a little ignorant bee, if, straying after
her eyes' desire, she suddenly longed after so
beauteous and lovely a nose, and fell headlong
upon it to suck out a sip of honey?"

Here and there in the King's sour visage two
or three honeylike gleams appeared, and in one

of the faint creases at the corners of his mouth it almost seemed, for half a moment, as though the vaguest shadow of a smile would break through. It could only mean that the King approved the shrewd little Bee's defense. But he straightway remembered his fierce anger, and with thundery visage, he said,

"And what else, O thou wanton one? I perceive thy lip's cunning! Thou gottest that tongue from none other than thy grandmother, Deborah the Prophetess, wife of Lapidoth—may she rest in glory."

And the Bee took to herself still more courage, and said,

"And even though I have sinned, is it not the glory of Kings to forgive transgression? So let the sin of thy handmaid's poor daughter be this day as small and petty in the King's sight as the smallness of her understanding and the shortness of her days; and, this once, be thou slow to anger against her. Who knoweth: the day may yet come when my lord the King will find pleasure and profit even in the like of me, the least in the land. Then will I make recompense to my lord the King."

These words so delighted the King's heart that his ill temper all but turned away from him, and with a laugh he answered and said,

"O thou brazen-faced one! Should the King find pleasure and profit in such as *thou!* Canst thou ever requite *him?* Off with thee, quickly, or if not . . . !"

The word was yet in the King's mouth and the little Bee spread her wings and was gone.

But the King, beginning to laugh, went on laughing until no strength remained in him, and by reason of his laughter he shook like a palm branch in the hand of the shaker; and holding his sides he called out,

"Oh! Stay me with raisins, comfort me with apples! Did ye hear? That little object would make recompense to the King . . . !"

And while the King was still lighthearted from laughter he forgave all the bees for the brave little Bee's sake, and he dismissed them all in peace.

And by the advice of the physicians the King anointed his nose with ointment and it healed, so that his nose became as it was aforetime. And as the days went by the King no more remembered the little Bee but forgot her.

. . .

And it came to pass after many days that the Queen of Sheba came from a far country with a

very great train, and bearing many presents, to
behold Solomon in his palace and to prove him
with hard questions (as it is written in the Scroll
of the Kings). And after she had tried him seven
and seventy times with all her knowledge and
her riddles and her many cunning wiles yet could
not prevail over him, she tested him at the last
also in this wise. Into the hands of the youths and
maidens which she had brought with her from
her own country, she put bunches of flowers, all
of them the work of men's hands, save only one,
which was the work of nature, and she arranged
them in rows before the King, and she said,

"Before thee, O King Solomon, in the hands of

the youths and maidens, are bunches of flowers; some of them are living flowers and some of them flowers made by men's hands. Do thou, O King, distinguish between them by their appearance."

Now the man-made flowers were marvelously perfect and complete, of cunning workmanship: in no wise did they seem different from flowers of the field and of the garden.

For a long space of time Solomon looked, and regarded them. But he could not tell how to distinguish between them. And it distressed him greatly and he felt himself in very evil plight.

Then, while he was hesitating, his ear, and his ear alone, caught the sound of a faint humming outside the window. The King turned his eyes thither and, suddenly, his face lit up. He whispered to the man on his right hand,

"Be quick! Open the window!"

The window was opened, and into the room there sped a swift bee which none saw save the King alone. The Bee straightway alighted on one of the bunches of flowers.

A little smile appeared on the King's lips and, to the amazement of the Queen of Sheba and all that stood there, he pointed to that bunch on which the Bee had alighted, and he called out gaily,

"That is the bunch of live flowers!"

Thus did the Bee requite the King.

. . .

That night Solomon added yet one more proverb to the proverbs of his wisdom which he wrote on a scroll:

Whoso despiseth a thing shall suffer thereby.

Riddles

NEAR A HIGHWAY a Peasant was sowing a field. Just then the Tsar rode by, stopped near the Peasant, and said:

"Godspeed, little Peasant!"

"Thank you, my good man!" (He did not know that he was speaking to the Tsar.)

"Do you earn much profit from this field?" asked the Tsar.

"If the harvest is good, I may make eighty rubles," replied the Peasant.

"What do you do with this money?" asked the Tsar.

"Twenty rubles go for taxes, twenty go for debts, twenty I give in loans, and twenty I throw out of the window," replied the Peasant.

"Explain to me, Brother, what debts you must pay, to whom you loan money, and why you throw money out of the window."

"Supporting my father is paying a debt; feed-

ing my son is lending money; feeding my daughter is throwing it out of the window," said the
Peasant.

"You speak the truth," said the Tsar. He gave
the Peasant a handful of silver coins, disclosed
that he was the Tsar and forbade the man to tell
these things to anyone outside of his presence. "No
matter who asks you, do not answer!"

The Tsar went to his capital and summoned
his boyars and generals. "Solve this riddle," he
said to them.

"On my way I saw a Peasant who was sowing
a field. I asked him what profit he earned from
it and what he did with his money and he answered that if the harvest was good he got eighty
rubles, and that he paid out twenty rubles in
taxes, twenty for debt, twenty as loans, and
twenty he threw out of the window. To him who
solves this riddle I will give great rewards and
great honors."

The boyars and generals thought and thought
but could not solve the riddle. But one Boyar hit
upon the idea of going to the Peasant with whom
the Tsar had spoken. He gave the Peasant a whole
pile of silver rubles and asked him:

"Tell me the answer to the Tsar's riddle."

The Peasant cast a glance at the money, took
it, and explained everything to the Boyar, who

returned to the Tsar and repeated the solution of the riddle.

The Tsar realized that the Peasant had not abided by the imperial command, and ordered that he be brought to court.

The Peasant appeared before the Tsar and at once admitted that he had told everything to the Boyar.

"Well, Brother, for such an offense I must order you put to death, and you have only yourself to thank for it."

"Your Majesty, I am not guilty of any offense, because I told everything to the Boyar in your presence," said the Peasant. As he said this, the Peasant drew from his pocket a silver ruble with the Tsar's likeness on it, and showed it to the Tsar.

"You speak the truth," said the Tsar. "This is my person." And he generously rewarded the Peasant and sent him home.

NOTES FROM THE STORYTELLER

The time listed for telling each story is an approximate one. The actual time may be shorter, longer, or the same as indicated. The skill of the storyteller, the natural pacing of the storyteller's speech, and most important the reaction of the listeners can affect the time it takes to tell any story at one particular telling.

1. *The Magpie and Her Children*
    TELLING TIME: 1 minute, 30 seconds
    AUDIENCE: Any age. Boys and girls. Will also appeal to an adult group.
    SOURCE: TALES OF LAUGHTER by Kate Douglas Wiggin and Nora Archibald Smith, c 1908, The McClure Co.

2. *The Frog and the Snake*
    TELLING TIME: 1 minute, 20 seconds
    AUDIENCE: 8 years and older. Boys and girls
    SOURCE: THE TALKING THRUSH by W. H. D. Rouse, c 1899, J. M. Dent and E. P. Dutton. Used by permission.

3. *Thirty-two Teeth*
    TELLING TIME: 1 minute
    AUDIENCE: 8 years and older. Boys and girls
    SOURCE: Adapted from story of same name in AN ARGOSY OF FABLES by Frederic Taber Cooper, c 1921, Frederick Stokes Co.

4. *The Fox and the Icicle*
    TELLING TIME: 30 seconds
    AUDIENCE: 8 years and older. Boys and girls
    SOURCE: AN ARGOSY OF FABLES by Frederic Taber Cooper, c 1921, Frederick Stokes Co.

5. *A Witty Answer*
    TELLING TIME: 1 minute
    AUDIENCE: 8 years and older. Boys and girls

SOURCE: Adapted from GEORGIAN FOLK TALES by Marjory Wardrop, c 1894, David Nutt in the Strand.

6. *Origin of Day and Night*

TELLING TIME: 1 minute, 30 seconds

AUDIENCE: Any age. Boys and girls. The group can be divided so that each side can say the Owl's word while the other side says the Rabbit's word.

SOURCE: This is a Menomini Indian tale from MYTHS AND LEGENDS OF THE MISSISSIPPI VALLEY AND THE GREAT LAKES by Katharine B. Judson, c 1914, A. C. McClurg Co.

7. *Manabush and the Moose*

TELLING TIME: 1 minute

AUDIENCE: 6 years and up. Boys and girls

SOURCE: Adapted from a Menomini Indian tale from MYTHS AND LEGENDS OF THE MISSISSIPPI VALLEY AND THE GREAT LAKES by Katharine B. Judson, c 1914, A. C. McClurg Co.

8. *The Box with Something Pretty in It*

TELLING TIME: 1 minute

AUDIENCE: All ages. Boys and girls

SOURCE: TALES OF LAUGHTER by Kate Douglas Wiggin and Nora Archibald Smith, c 1908, The McClure Co.

9. *The Arab and His Camel*

TELLING TIME: 30 seconds

AUDIENCE: All ages. Boys and girls

SOURCE: Adapted from story of the same name in AN ARGOSY OF FABLES by Frederic Taber Cooper, c 1921, Frederick A. Stokes.

10. *The Tail*

TELLING TIME: 1 minute

AUDIENCE: All ages. Boys and girls

SOURCE: TALES OF LAUGHTER by Kate Douglas Wiggin and Nora Archibald Smith, c 1908, The McClure Co.

11. *Foolish Mother Goat*

TELLING TIME: 4 minutes

AUDIENCE: 8 years and older. Boys and girls

SOURCE: THE MAGIC BIRD OF CHOMO-LUNG-MA by Sybille Noel, c 1931, Doubleday, Doran & Co.

12. *The Most Frugal of Men*

TELLING TIME: 3 minutes

AUDIENCE: 8 years and up. Boys and girls. Will appeal
to an adult group.

SOURCE: Adapted from story of same name in TALES
OF LAUGHTER by Kate Douglas Wiggin and
Nora Archibald Smith, c 1908, The McClure Co.

13. *The Crow and the Peacock*
TELLING TIME: 2 minutes, 30 seconds
AUDIENCE: All ages. Boys and girls
SOURCES: AN ARGOSY OF FABLES by Frederick
Taber Cooper, c 1921, Frederick A. Stokes.

14. *The Shepherd Boy Who Was Wiser Than the King*
TELLING TIME: 2 minutes
AUDIENCE: All ages. Boys and girls. Will also appeal
to an adult group.
SOURCE: Adapted from *The Little Shepherd Boy* from
TALES OF LAUGHTER by Kate Douglas Wiggin
and Nora Archibald Smith, c 1908, The McClure Co.

15. *How the Chipmunk Came to Be*
TELLING TIME: 2 minutes
AUDIENCE: 8 years and older. Boys particularly
SOURCE: Retold from *How the Chipmunk Came* in A
BOOK OF INDIAN TALES, ed. by Charles Erskine
Scott Wood, c 1929, The Vanguard Press. Used by
permission.

16. *The Best of the Bargain*
TELLING TIME: 4 minutes
AUDIENCE: All ages. Boys and girls
SOURCE: HAJJI BABA OF ISPAHAN by James
Morier, published by Bentley, c 1851.

17. *The Parrot and the Parson*
TELLING TIME: 3 minutes
AUDIENCE: 8 years and up. Boys and girls
SOURCE: As adapted from THE TALKING THRUSH
by W. H. D. Rouse, c 1899, J. M. Dent and E. P.
Dutton. Used by permission.

18. *The Lost Camel*
TELLING TIME: 3 minutes
AUDIENCE: All ages. Boys and girls. Boys particularly
SOURCE: A story by Oliver Goldsmith from AN
ARGOSY OF FABLES by Frederic Taber Cooper,
c 1921, Frederick A. Stokes.

19. *Jupiter and the Horse*
TELLING TIME: 2 minutes, 30 seconds
AUDIENCE: All ages. Boys and girls

SOURCE: AN ARGOSY OF FABLES by Frederic
Taber Cooper, c 1921, Frederick A. Stokes.

20. *How the Fog Came*
TELLING TIME: 3 minutes
AUDIENCE: 10 years and up. Boys and girls
SOURCE: Retold from story of same name in ESKIMO
FOLK TALES, collected by Knud Rasmussen, edi-
ted and rendered into English by W. Worster,
c 1921, Gyldendal. Used by permission.

21. *The Tiger and the Frog*
TELLING TIME: 7 minutes
AUDIENCE: 8 years and up. Boys and girls
SOURCE: Retold from story of the same name in THE
MAGIC BIRD OF CHOMO-LUNG-MA by Sybille
Noel, c 1931, by Doubleday, Doran and Co.

22. *The Wise Old Shepherd*
TELLING TIME: 8 minutes
AUDIENCE: 8 years and up. Boys and girls
SOURCE: As adapted from THE TALKING THRUSH
by W. H. D. Rouse, c 1899, J. M. Dent Co. and
E. P. Dutton. Used by permission.

23. *The Wily Tortoise*
TELLING TIME: 2 minutes
AUDIENCE: All ages. Boys and girls
SOURCE: As adapted from THE TALKING THRUSH
by W. H. D. Rouse, c 1899, J. M. Dent and E. P.
Dutton. Used by permission.

24. *How the Coyote Stole Fire for the Klamaths*
TELLING TIME: 5 minutes
AUDIENCE: 8 years and up. Boys and girls. Boys in
particular
SOURCE: Retold from story of the same name in A
BOOK OF INDIAN TALES by Charles Erskine
Scott Wood, c 1929, The Vanguard Press. Used by
permission.

25. *The Cat and the Sparrows*
TELLING TIME: 5 minutes
AUDIENCE: All ages. Boys and girls. Girls particularly
SOURCE: As adapted from THE TALKING THRUSH
by W. H. D. Rouse, c 1899, J. M. Dent and E. P.
Dutton. Used by permission.

26. *The Race*
TELLING TIME: 3 minutes, 30 seconds
AUDIENCE: All ages. Boys and girls. Boys particularly

SOURCE: BLACKFOOT LODGE TALES by George Bird Grinnell, c 1920, George Bird Grinnell, published by Charles Scribner's.

27. *Why the Possum's Tail Is Bare*
TELLING TIME: 3 minutes
AUDIENCE: All ages. Boys and girls
SOURCE: A Cherokee Indian tale from MYTHS AND LEGENDS OF THE MISSISSIPPI VALLEY AND THE GREAT LAKES by Katharine B. Judson, c 1914, A. C. McClurg.

28. *The Man Who Ate His Wives*
TELLING TIME: 4 minutes
AUDIENCE: 10 years and up. Boys and girls
SOURCE: Retold from *Imarasugssuaq, Who Ate His Wives* in ESKIMO FOLK TALES, collected by Knud Rasmussen. Edited and rendered into English by W. Worster, c 1921 Gyldendal. Used by permission.

29. *The Giant and the Dwarf*
TELLING TIME: 5 minutes
AUDIENCE: All ages. Boys and girls
SOURCE: Retold from *The Strong Man and the Dwarf* in GEORGIAN FOLK TALES by Marjory Wardrop, c 1894, David Nutt in the Strand.

30. *The Monkey and the Heron*
TELLING TIME: 8 minutes
AUDIENCE: All ages. Boys and girls
SOURCE: Retold from story of the same name in THE MAGIC BIRD OF CHOMO-LUNG-MA by Sybille Noel, c 1931, Doubleday, Doran and Co.

31. *The Ghost Who Was Afraid of Being Bagged*
TELLING TIME: 7 minutes
AUDIENCE: 8 years and up. Boys and girls
SOURCE: As adapted from FOLK-TALES OF BENGAL by Lal Behari Day, c 1883, Macmillan and Co., Ltd.

32. *The Wolf and the Blacksmith*
TELLING TIME: 7 minutes
AUDIENCE: All ages. Boys and girls
SOURCE: As adapted from THE MASTER WIZARD AND OTHER POLISH TALES. Trans. from the Polish by Josephine B. Bernhard. Rev. and adapted by E. Frances Le Valley. Copyright 1934 by Joseph-

ine B. Bernhard and E. Frances Le Valley. Published by Alfred A. Knopf.

33. *The Story of Yukpachen*
   TELLING TIME: 5 minutes
   AUDIENCE: 8 years and up. Boys and girls. Boys particularly
   SOURCE: As adapted from the story of the same name
   in THE MAGIC BIRD OF CHOMO-LUNG-MA
   by Sybille Noel, c 1931, Doubleday, Doran and Co.

34. *Yehl Outwits Kanukh*
   TELLING TIME: 7 minutes
   AUDIENCE: 8 years and up. Boys and girls. Boys par-
   ticularly
   SOURCE: Retold from *How Yehl Outwitted Kanukh
   and Gave Fresh Water to the Thlinkets* in A BOOK
   OF INDIAN TALES by Charles Erskine Scott
   Wood, c 1929, The Vanguard Press. Used by per-
   mission.

35. *How the Devil Was Outsmarted by the Man*
   TELLING TIME: 5 minutes
   AUDIENCE: All ages. Boys and girls
   SOURCE: As adapted from *How the Devil Contended
   with the Man* from BEYOND THE GIANT
   MOUNTAINS by Adolf Wenig. Translated by
   Lillian P. Mokrejs, c 1923, by Lillian P. Mokrejs.
   Published by Houghton Mifflin.

36. *Teeth and No-Teeth*
   TELLING TIME: 2 minutes
   AUDIENCE: All ages. Boys and girls. Will also appeal
   to an adult group.
   SOURCE: GEORGIAN FOLK TALES by Marjory
   Wardrop, c 1894, David Nutt in the Strand.

37. *How the Hodja Outwits the Shah Ali*
   TELLING TIME: 4 minutes
   AUDIENCE: 8 years and up. Boys and girls
   SOURCE: As adapted from *The King and the Sage*
   from GEORGIAN FOLK TALES by Marjory War-
   drop, c 1894, David Nutt in the Strand.

38. *Heavy Collar and the Ghost Woman*
   TELLING TIME: 18 minutes
   AUDIENCE: 8 years and up. Boys and girls
   SOURCE: Retold from story of the same name in
   BLACKFOOT LODGE TALES by George Bird

Grinnell, c 1920, George Bird Grinnell. Published
by Charles Scribner's.

39. *The Bee*

TELLING TIME: 13 minutes

AUDIENCE: All ages. Boys and girls. Will also appeal
to adult groups.

SOURCE: AND IT CAME TO PASS told by Kayyim
Nahman Bialik; translated by Herbert Danby, c
1938, Hebrew Publishing Co.

40. *Riddles*

TELLING TIME: 2 minutes

AUDIENCE: 8 years and up. Boys and girls. Will also
appeal to adult groups.

SOURCE: RUSSIAN FAIRY TALES, edited by Norbert Guterman, c 1945, Pantheon.